It took every ounce of his courage to say his next words.

"I can't do it without you."

"But you're always so brave."

"People only see my adventurous spirit. They don't see beyond that to the real me. The real me gets as scared as the next guy. I just don't ever talk about it. To anyone. I need a friend."

Did she nod her head? The slight movement may or may not have been agreement. The deliberate nod that followed removed his doubt.

"I'm in." She clasped her other hand over his. "I need you, too."

She needed him.

A rumbling in his soul awakened a long-dormant love for her. The strength of it frightened him, but he would never back away from her again. No matter what she said.

"I'm in, too."

I think I'm falling in love with Sophie all over again. And I can never let her know.

Angel Moore fell in love with romance in elementary school when she read the story of Robin Hood and Maid Marian. Inspired by her husband, who taught her everything she knows about living happily ever after, Angel writes stories of faith and a hope she knows is real because of God's goodness to her. When not writing, she's probably reading a book or watching way too much television. After all, every love story is research, right? Find her at www.angelmoorebooks.com.

Books by Angel Moore

Love Inspired

Their Family Arrangement

Love Inspired Historical

Conveniently Wed
The Marriage Bargain
The Rightful Heir
Husband by Arrangement
A Ready-Made Texas Family

Visit the Author Profile page at Harlequin.com.

Their Family Arrangement

Angel Moore

LOVE INSPIRED
INSPIRATIONAL ROMANCE

LOVE INSPIRED®
INSPIRATIONAL ROMANCE

ISBN-13: 978-1-335-48882-4

Their Family Arrangement

Copyright © 2021 by Angelissa J. Moore

This edition published by arrangement with Harlequin Books S.A.

For questions and comments about the quality of this book, please contact us at CustomerService@Harlequin.com.

Love Inspired
22 Adelaide St. West, 40th Floor
Toronto, Ontario M5H 4E3, Canada
www.Harlequin.com

Printed in U.S.A.

Pure religion and undefiled before God and the Father is this, To visit the fatherless and widows in their affliction, and to keep himself unspotted from the world.
—*James* 1:27

To Melody, who brings me joy and laughter.
Thank you for inspiring Jade's character and
lending her your name.

To Christ, who continues to bring me hope.

Thank you, Kathleen Y'Barbo, for your help
sorting through the Texas legal information.
Accurate depictions are due to you.
All mistakes are my own.

Chapter One

"Judge Carlisle has consistently granted guardianship of children to married couples. It's practically become a trademark of his time on the bench. Since the two of you are only friends, I don't see this ending well. And he's set the hearing for tomorrow morning."

The lawyer's words shocked Kevin Lane. He hadn't had time to change out of the suit he'd worn to the joint funeral of his best friends and already the future of their children was in jeopardy. "But Logan and Caitlyn asked us to be guardians for Jade and Carter before they included us in their wills."

Sophie Owens set a tray with a pitcher of water and glasses on the dining room table, then took a seat opposite Kevin.

He still felt like an interloper in Logan and Caitlyn's house. To keep from adding to the turmoil of the young children's lives, he and Sophie had stayed in their home since the accident. Sophie's mom had been there to help, day and night. "We haven't had time to discuss the details and make permanent plans, but we're both committed to joint guardianship of the children."

Jackson Yarbrough waved off Sophie's offer of a glass of water. "Judge Carlisle wants children to be placed in permanent situations as quickly as possible, and in his experience, that's best with married couples." Jackson might be a good lawyer—and a friend—but he seemed to be narrowing their options instead of increasing them.

"But we're who their parents wanted." Sophie tapped the table with two fingers while her frown emphasized the depth of her thoughts. She sat up in an instant. "My mother is a friend of Judge Carlisle's wife. Do you think that would be a validation of our character to him?"

The lawyer shook his head. "No. If his wife had shared anything negative about you or Kevin, that might harm you, but a friendship with your mother wouldn't be enough for him to give you extra consideration. He'll likely still insist on a married couple. If you two got married, you'd be ideal guardians." He shrugged as if the statement wasn't ludicrous.

Kevin couldn't believe what he was hearing. "You're seriously suggesting we need to get married?" Marriage? The only reason Kevin and Sophie were even friends was because of Logan and Caitlyn. It hadn't been easy to get beyond their past. They'd done it, or at least he liked to think they had. "We have every intention of raising Jade and Carter. They're safe with us. They know and love us, and we love them. That love should count more than anything."

Sophie leaned forward in her chair. "Absolutely. It's hard enough to lose their parents. They can't lose us, too. No matter what we have to do…" The end of her statement had slowed as if the weight of it was changing something in her perspective.

He didn't like where this was going. Was she considering Jackson's suggestion? "No, Sophie." After all these years he could always tell what she was thinking. And right now she was thinking marriage. Kevin pushed his chair away from the table and stood. "We can't."

She shook her head and held up one hand to stop him from speaking. "Wait. It's not something I'd ever suggest, but if we must—"

Kevin looked at Jackson. "Let's ask for a different judge." He poured himself a glass of water and drank it as if quenching his thirst could solve his problems.

Jackson shook his head. "Judge Carlisle is the only judge who handles family law in Gran Colina. Logan and Caitlyn were so young that I never imagined they'd be gone so soon. I warned them about the judge's quirks, but since he'd announced his early retirement before we finalized the wills, we didn't think he'd be a factor. Everyone in the legal community was surprised last month when he decided to stay on for the rest of his term. We were supposed to meet next week to see if they wanted to revise the wills."

"We can go to court in the next town." Kevin wouldn't give up. There had to be a way to avoid this judge.

Sophie's eyes met his. He saw a reflection of the sadness that had filled her gaze when she'd broken up with him in the summer after her senior year of high school.

Kevin's mind scrambled for a solution that wouldn't find him telling her how badly she'd hurt him all those years before. At one time he couldn't have imagined marrying anyone else. He'd never gotten over the loss of her. In fact, he no longer wanted to marry anyone. Ever.

Jackson shot down his idea. "He's the only probate judge for the whole county. The population of Gran Colina and our neighbors doesn't justify needing more than one judge for these cases. And he isn't all you have to deal with. There are background checks and details for the guardianship. Even if he grants you immediate guardianship, it would be temporary pending an investigation by the court."

"An investigation?" Sophie's question was soft, her tone troubled.

Kevin set his empty glass on the table, hard. So hard that she jumped in her chair. "There's nothing to investigate, Sophie. It's all a bunch of court mumbo jumbo that has nothing to do with what Logan and Caitlyn asked us to do for those kids." He pointed toward the hallway that led to Jade's and Carter's bedrooms. He'd made a promise to Logan, and nothing was going to prevent him from raising those kids. They were as much a part of his world as any child would ever be. He'd been in their lives from the beginning.

He and Sophie. Logan had been his best friend, and Caitlyn had been Sophie's. It was natural they'd been asked to serve as guardians. What wasn't natural was two lives taken at such a young age and leaving those precious kids behind.

Jackson interfered. Again. "It's not mumbo jumbo, Kevin. We've all known each other since middle school. I'm only trying to help. I know you're upset, but you can't go into the courtroom tomorrow and let the emotions you're feeling show. The processes of the court are in place for the protection of every child. More kids than you can imagine come before Judge Carlisle without the care and provision Logan and Caitlyn gave to Jade and Carter. I assure you their wishes will be considered." Kevin hated that Jackson was talking to him in what must be his lawyer tone.

Kevin's shoulders slumped. "I'll be calm in court. This is just too much. It hasn't been a week since the accident that took them. Anyone would be overwhelmed. I haven't figured out how I'm going to balance my work with raising kids. It's hard enough for a couple. I don't know where to begin." He drew in a harsh breath. "How will they cope? To be so little and lose your parents?"

Jackson shrugged. "That's likely the argument the judge will use against you. It's important that you don't do anything that will give him cause for concern about you or Sophie."

Sophie turned to Jackson. "What's the bottom line? Are you saying that you don't think Judge Carlisle will let us keep the kids if we aren't married, even though there's no law that says we have to be? Isn't he supposed to operate according to the law?"

Kevin wasn't surprised by her thoughtful approach to this unbelievable conversation. She carefully planned everything in her life, while he tackled any situation at full speed. Her patience would be infuriating if he didn't know it was just who she was.

Jackson nodded. "I've never seen a case where he let it happen."

Kevin struggled to control his grief and frustration. "Why do we have to go to court tomorrow? Can't we have a minute to mourn before some judge jumps into the middle of our business? This is too quick, Jackson."

"I know it seems like that, but I've been in his courtroom often enough to know that it's not uncommon for orphans to be placed on the day their parents die."

Kevin gripped the back of the chair he'd vacated. "They aren't orphans." He hated to think of the children like that. "I mean, I know they are in the legal sense of the word, but they have me and Sophie. We're taking care of them."

Sophie stood, walked around the table and took Kevin's hand. "Let's go out on the back porch for a few minutes."

She pointed at the two baby monitors on the kitchen island. "Jackson, the kids are napping. Will you come get us if they wake up?"

"Sure." He pulled out his phone. "I can give you guys a few minutes, but I've got to get everything together, and we don't have much time."

"We'll be quick." She stepped through the back door, and Kevin followed her outside.

"Can you believe this?" He pushed his hands through his hair and went to lean against the porch railing.

"It's not what I expected, either." She stood beside him facing the open backyard. "But *we* have to make up our minds about what to do, or that judge is going to decide for us."

He paced the porch from one end to the other, stopping to lift a finger. They could tell the judge it would confuse the kids if they married. He shook his head and turned to pace in the opposite direction. If that sounded feeble in his mind, how much worse would it sound out loud in court?

When he would have passed her again, Sophie reached out and snagged him by the arm. "I can't think if you keep walking back and forth."

"Movement gets my brain going." He pulled free of her grasp and walked to the end of the porch. There wasn't anything in the Bible he could think of that would make it against their faith to marry. Would they be ridiculous to even consider marriage? The Bible spoke of helping widows and orphans, but surely God knew he was more than willing to help the kids without having to marry Sophie.

Then an unwelcome and scary thought crossed his mind. What if Sophie found someone and fell in love? She could marry and move away from Gran Colina. Would she want to take the kids with her? That would devastate them all over again. And he already loved those little ones so much. He couldn't lose them. Now— or ever.

He pivoted and came to stand in front of her. "I have no ideas. This cannot be happening. What century is this judge living in? Single people raise children all the time. It's about the commitment to the child."

"I guess he's thinking the kids will be better off in one home with the same kind of security their parents provided. Maybe because we lead separate lives he won't see how we can work together for the kids. Honestly, Kevin, I'm scared." She looked up at him and drew her lips inward.

Kevin recognized that expression. It only happened when she needed to gather her strength to say something she knew he didn't want to hear. "What do you think we should do?" He braced himself.

"I can raise them both alone." And there it was. The exact opposite of anything he'd ever agree to.

"No. That's not what their parents wanted." He took a breath to keep the pain of his childhood memories from rising to the surface. Raised by babysitters and left alone too many times by a single mother who'd never wanted him had left lifelong scars.

Sophie loved Jade and Carter as much as he did and would never treat them like that, but he wouldn't leave her to do the work alone. "They've lost their parents. They're going to face challenges beyond our imagination. We can't let them struggle without a stable environment. If either of us takes on both of them we'd have to hire sitters or—at best—a nanny who won't love them like we do. They deserve all the support we can give them. We promised their parents."

He would *not* break that promise. It was the biggest commitment he'd ever made—except for the commitment he'd made to Sophie in his heart before he'd bought an engagement ring. A ring he'd never given her because she'd ended their relationship three weeks before he'd planned to propose. A commitment she'd never known about.

He wouldn't let Sophie—or anyone else—keep him from fulfilling his promise to Logan and Caitlyn.

The determination in Sophie's face never wavered. "Sitters are inevitable. We both work."

"I don't think a judge who wants married couples as guardians would agree to one of us raising them alone. We'll have to find a way to arrange our lives around the kids."

Just not marriage. The idea of marrying Sophie in order to give Jade and Carter a family, without sharing the love he'd treasured in their youth, boggled his mind.

"You know we can't just share a house." She blushed. "My mother would have a stroke if she thought I was living with a man. Helping with the children wasn't her only reason for staying here every night."

He chuckled. "Your mother? Do you think she's our biggest problem right now?"

"Not our biggest problem." Sophie winced. "But she lives two miles away from here. I'd never hear the end of it." She shrugged. "And, honestly, I wouldn't feel right about it. Call me old-fashioned, but it goes against my faith. People would think we're living together without being married. I'm concerned that could hurt the children, too."

Sophie was right. They shared the same faith. He'd never do anything to hurt the kids. Or her.

Plus, his reputation in the community was important to the success of his business. He'd worked hard to gain the respect of the people of Gran Colina—no easy task for a man who never knew his father and was left to his own devices by an absentee mom.

Their small town could be set aflame with gossip in an instant. Carter and Jade needed guardians who were esteemed, not reviled, by others. Kevin's livelihood and the children's financial provision depended on it.

Jackson opened the back door of the house. "The kids are waking up." He checked his watch. "I really need to get to the office to handle the details of this. Did you come to any decisions about how you want to proceed?"

"No." Sophie walked past Jackson into the house. "There's so much to consider."

"Mama." Carter's sweet cries came through one of the baby monitors on the kitchen island.

"I need to see about him." Kevin walked around Jackson. "Sophie and I will talk more after the kids go to sleep tonight. Can we call you first thing in the morning?"

"Make it early." The lawyer pushed the paperwork into his case. "I've left a copy of the will for each of you. I'd recommend you both get on the same page and act as a team in court. Judge Carlisle will be easier to work with if you're united."

Kevin threw up a hand to acknowledge Jackson as he stepped into the hallway that led to Carter's room. As he entered the nursery, he heard Sophie thank the lawyer for coming.

Carter stood at the rail of the gray crib and laughed. "K." He stretched out chubby arms to Kevin and squealed. "K."

Kevin's heart melted. Again. The sight of this trusting child reaching for him brought fresh tears to his eyes. "I'm here, little buddy." He picked Carter up and gave him a hug. "I'm here."

He walked to the changing table and used a toy to distract the happy child while he changed his diaper. Wrestling a bear cub might be easier. None of the equipment in his sporting goods store could match the little guy, but Kevin had spent enough time with Carter to know the little tricks that kept the baby from winning the tussling match.

The bond the children shared with him and Sophie would help them all to heal. If marriage to Sophie—as friends and co-parents—was the only way to keep them together, he knew he might have to consider it. But not before they explored all their other options.

Carter wrapped his tiny arms around Kevin's neck and squeezed.

"Okay, little man. Snack time." He headed back to the kitchen, praying with all his heart that he and Sophie could come up with the right solution to give these children the best life possible in light of their circumstances.

Sorrow filled him with more motivation than any adrenaline pumping through his veins for a new sporting adventure ever had. The nerve it took to jump from the platform at the top of a zip line paled in comparison to the mental fortitude and determination it would take to conquer the problem of raising Carter and his big sister. Especially if that meant marriage. As much as Sophie hated risks and the unknown, he knew this was worse for her than him. Helping her face whatever happened tomorrow would help them all in the long run.

He hoped.

Later that evening, Sophie lifted Carter from the tub and handed him to Kevin. "Here you go, little man. Uncle K will take it from here." Kevin's height and athletic build made the generous space feel cramped. If they hadn't spent so much time together in Logan and Caitlyn's house over the years, his nearness might be awkward. At this point, she was just grateful for his help.

"Thanks, Sophie." Kevin wrapped the wet, wriggling baby in a hooded towel adorned with puppy dog ears and left the large bathroom the kids shared.

Sophie, on her knees by the tub, reached for Jade. "Okay, princess. Let's make sure all the shampoo is out of your hair."

"Soapy, I wanna wear my princess pj's." Jade used the pet name she'd given Sophie when she was too young to pronounce her name. It always made Sophie's heart smile to hear it.

"Okay. The pink ones or the yellow ones?" Sophie rinsed the bubbles from under Jade's chin.

"Pink!" Jade sloshed a wave of water over the edge of the tub.

"Whoa, there. Let's get you out before we have to swim out of here."

Sophie bundled Jade into a towel and went to the child's pink-and-white bedroom. She could hear Kevin talking to Carter in the other room while she helped Jade get into her favorite pajamas. The way Carter babbled with Kevin was adorable. At fourteen months, most of the words were garbled, but the laughter in his voice gave Sophie hope that one day these kids would be okay again.

Happy baby giggles belied the heavy choices she and Kevin had to make tonight. Her mind reeled as her thoughts swung like a pendulum between rationalizing the idea of marrying for the sake of the kids or living separate lives with the possibility of losing their rights to care for the children.

Where did the answer lie? Kevin's daring nature scared her. It always had, but now two children were involved. They didn't need another accidental death in their lives, but risk defined Kevin. He never met a challenge he didn't tackle.

It was the reason she'd broken off their relationship the summer before she'd left for college. Losing her father in a motorcycle accident during her senior year of high school had taken all the bravery out of her. When Kevin had been hurt that summer, the sadness of her father's death had threatened to overwhelm her again. She'd chosen to live a safe, if unadventurous, life ever since. Risk no longer held any fascination for her.

As she brushed Jade's hair and gave silly answers to her constant babbling, Sophie silently begged God for a logical solution that would satisfy the judge.

She finished getting Jade ready for bed, and they walked down the short hallway to Carter's bedroom.

"Someone wants to say good-night prayers with her little brother." Sophie sat on the stool in front of the rocker where Kevin held Carter in his lap.

Jade climbed up to join her brother and tugged his hands together. "You have to hold your hands like Daddy told us." At only three, Jade had already mastered her big-sister role.

"P'ay?" Carter smiled at Jade, and ripples formed on the surface of the puddle that once was Sophie's heart. These two little people had melted it with their love and the sadness of the plight they were too young to understand.

"Yes." Jade nodded. "Now close your eyes." She closed her eyes and opened them immediately. "And no peeking." She looked from Kevin to Sophie, and then to Carter.

"Okay." Kevin laughed and closed his eyes.

"Dear Lord." Jade always started her prayers the same way. If Sophie knew anything in her soul, she knew Jesus would hear this child's prayer. "Help me and Carter be good. We're sad, and sometimes that makes me want to not be good."

Sophie dared to take a glance at Kevin and found him watching her. Their shared look let her know that no matter what happened in court tomorrow morning, the two of them would take care of these children for the rest of their lives.

"Help Mommy and Daddy, 'cause they don't like to be away from us so long." Jade gave a deep sigh. "I don't like it neither. Amen."

One week seemed an eternity to children. To Sophie, the last few days had flown by and dragged at the same time. Loss had filled their lives, yet Jade's concern for her parents filled the child's prayer.

Lord, thank You for the faith Logan and Caitlyn instilled in their children. Help me and Kevin continue

*the training they started. Being a parent is harder than
I ever imagined.*

Jade slid out of the chair. "Now we have to read a
story." She went to the bookcase, pulled a book from the
top of the stack and handed it to Sophie. "You can read
this. Mommy always starts at the big'innin'."

"Is this your favorite?" Sophie pulled Jade onto her
lap and opened the well-worn book.

"It makes me and Carter laugh when Mommy does
funny voices." Jade snuggled against her, and Sophie
didn't know if she'd be able to see the words through the
tears that filled her eyes. Logan and Caitlyn should be
here. A flash flood on a stormy night had robbed these
precious children of their loving parents.

She sniffed and cleared her throat. It had to be done.
The kids needed her and Kevin to be strong. The first
three pages held a familiar character who talked in
rhymes and silly words. Sophie chose a high-pitched
tone and mimicked the facial expressions of the character. Carter and Jade giggled.

Sophie turned the book so the kids could see the page,
and Kevin picked up the reading with the next illustrated
animal. By the time they finished the book, everyone
was feeling silly and relaxed.

"Give your brother a kiss." Sophie lifted Jade to reach
Carter.

"Night-night, Carter." Jade put a sweet kiss on his
cheek. "Night-night, Uncle K." She held up her small
hand for his high five.

"Good night, sweet girl." Kevin's voice was thick and
heavy. Sophie knew he was as moved as she was by the
family scene they'd just played a part in.

She kissed Carter on the top of the head and ruffled his wispy hair with her hand. "Sweet dreams."

After Jade was tucked into her bed, Sophie went back to the kitchen. Kevin stood at the sink loading the dishwasher.

"Thank you." She slid onto a stool at the island. "I'm exhausted."

"Me, too." He added the detergent, closed the machine and turned it on. "Who knew parenting was so tiring." The gentle swishing of water in the dishwasher made her eyes droop.

She chuckled. "I think everyone but us."

He sobered. "Grief is a heavier load, though."

Sophie nodded. "I guess we need to talk about tomorrow."

Kevin offered her a cup of coffee, which she refused, so he handed her a bottle of water and asked if they could sit in the living area.

She settled into the end corner of the comfy sectional, and he sat in the chair Logan had insisted on keeping after he and Caitlyn had married. They both stared off into oblivion, lost in their own thoughts for a few minutes.

"This is incomprehensible." Sophie's mind had twisted and turned with every conceivable possibility, and she still couldn't imagine the kids being taken from them. "We are their guardians. No judge should have the right to take them away after their parents made their wishes known."

"I agree, but Jackson's concern has me worried."

"It's all that's been on my mind since he left." Sophie twisted the top off the water bottle. "I'd like to go into court as if everything will be handled according to the will." The way Kevin had resisted Jackson's cautions about the judge's preference for married couples, she was afraid he wouldn't be willing to get married even if she asked him to. He was as stubborn as he was adventurous. That daring nature made him the last person she'd ever want to marry. But today she found herself considering things she'd never have imagined before taking on the responsibility of guardianship.

He nodded. "Okay, but shouldn't we have an explanation for how we're going to manage joint guardianship in case he asks? And what about the house and who'll live where?"

"Well, since the will names both of us as trustees over everything for the kids—the house, insurance money and all assets—that should take care of their college. I'm sure Jackson can help us through the paperwork on that. Do you think we should sell the house and put the money in the trust?"

"We could, but will the kids adjust better if they stay here?"

"That might be best." Sophie grabbed a notebook from the kitchen counter and came back to the sofa. "A logical list with check boxes always helps me." She hoped it would ease her worries now, but she doubted it would. Pen in hand, she made notes as they talked. "I can keep Caitlyn's SUV. You can use the insurance money from Logan's car when it's settled." She shuddered and stretched her neck. "I can't believe we're rattling off their possessions like a grocery list."

"I know, and I hate it. But we've got to work through it." Kevin scrubbed his hands across his eyes. He blew out a forceful breath before he continued. "We need to figure out how to handle raising them together. Who takes care of what in their day-to-day schedules, and who takes them to the park or out for ice cream."

Sophie smiled at the thought of Kevin trudging to the park with the kids. "We may need to do that together. Both of them at the same time is a handful."

Kevin held his hands out, palms up. "A handful we're going to have to learn to manage."

"You're right." She shrugged. "We'll have to work together on how to spend the money for them, and we seem to be in agreement about that. What if we decide on an amount for a monthly allotment from the insurance to use for them?"

"It's so much to think about."

She agreed and tapped her pen against the page. "It's hard enough to budget in ordinary circumstances. This grief is making it surreal."

"It's like I can't breathe sometimes." He pressed his fist against his chest and closed his eyes.

"Me, too." Sophie leaned forward and put her hand on his knee. "I don't know how I'd be managing if you weren't here. We'll help each other through this."

He covered her hand with his. "They were right to choose both of us. It's too much for one person to bear."

The comfort of his hand on hers reminded her of happier days. Days when they'd laughed and enjoyed every possible moment together. They'd been so young and convinced the love they had for one another would protect them from all tragedy or pain. It hadn't been true, but it had been sweet.

She slid her hand away. They could handle the children together, and the logistics of co-parenting, but she couldn't rely on him for her comfort.

She cleared her throat and hoped to shift the focus

back to the tasks at hand. "I've got some budgeting software that I use in my accounting business and for my personal finances. Do you want me to create a tentative budget so we can sit down together and adjust it to work for both of us?"

He leaned back in the chair, his expression guarded, and answered her. "That's a good idea."

They worked through several financial details before the wind went out of Sophie's sails. "I know why you don't want to put the kids in day care, but we need to talk about it. Most families have to do it. We both need time to work. But it's a big expense, and being out of their home during the day will make them miss Caitlyn more. It's complicated, but I don't think we can just dismiss it."

"Is there something else we can do?" Kevin shrugged. "I have to be at the store at least five days a week, but everything inside of me hates the thought of putting them in day care or leaving them with a sitter."

Sophie looked around the living area. Toy bins were tucked on the bottom shelves that flanked the fireplace. Pictures of the happy family stood on the upper shelves. The Christmas card they'd sent out just a few weeks ago held a place of honor in the center of the display. Everything about the room resonated with a sense of home and family.

She hated the thought of packing the kids into her car every morning and taking them off to a place where they could be lost in the crowd. "Caitlyn had the perfect setup here with her office just off the kitchen. I run my business from home and love it, but I had no idea how important it was for her to be here with the kids. We talked about it when she decided to stay home after

Jade was born. It didn't sink in for me that it would matter so much.

"I guess I can try keeping the kids home with me. It will take some adjustments to my schedule, but I'm willing to give it a go. My clientele is a mix of people who come to me and people I go out to meet. We'd need someone to watch them when I have to go out."

"There's no way I could do anything like that. My store is no place for kids to spend their days. There are too many things they could get into."

"If I work here from Caitlyn's office, it would be what they're both used to."

"How could you work? You'd never get anything done."

"Caitlyn put in a lot of her work hours after Logan came home from work." She shook her head. The more she tried to figure out what they needed to do, the more she realized how *much* they had to figure out. "I know there's no perfect solution to any of our choices. Maybe you can come here on the days I have to go out to meet clients." Sophie sighed. "I thought we'd have more time to make the decisions."

Kevin ran both hands through his unruly hair. "I did, too. I can't believe it's been almost a week. We'd have been lost without your mom's help."

"The shock of it is what got me the most. I feel like I'm on autopilot, going through the motions but not really getting everything done." She drew a flower in the margin of the list she'd made. The mindless doodle couldn't free her mind of its troubles.

Kevin moved to the edge of the chair. "We can take our time with the rest of it, but apparently this judge isn't going to be flexible about getting the kids settled."

He finished his coffee and put the mug on the table by Logan's chair. "In a way, I understand it. It's probably best for them to be settled immediately and not have to adjust more than once."

"So we're agreed?" Sophie said. "We go into court tomorrow sticking to our ground about following the provisions of Logan and Caitlyn's wills for us to share guardianship of the children. We'll have to make the judge see how committed we are to the kids. That should get him off the silly notion that we need to be married to be good guardians."

"I hope so. I'll call Jackson in the morning, so he'll know how we want to proceed before we arrive in court. He'll have to convince the judge that we're committed to the kids but need more time to handle all the details." He nodded and pushed himself out of the chair. "I'm going to bed if you think that's all we need to handle tonight. I haven't slept well since the accident."

"Me, either." She stood and stretched her back. "I'm going to try to work for a while. I've gotten behind over the last few days. Most of my clients need their numbers by the thirty-first. Taxes wait for no one." She picked up her empty water bottle and the notepad covered with her checklist and nervous drawings. "Mom will be here soon. I asked her to stay with the kids tomorrow while we go to court."

He stilled and asked, "Do you think she'd be willing to keep them while we work? If we had an option besides day care, I'd feel better about the possibility of things going our way with the judge."

Sophie knew he respected her mom. His own mother had moved to Florida as soon as he'd graduated from high school and severed almost all communication with him. Sophie was certain the lack of care he'd received from her strengthened his resolve to do his best for Jade and Carter.

"No. I wish she could, but she's worked full-time since my dad passed. It's not just about the money. They give her benefits at the bank. She took vacation days to be here and help us. I think she's off for the rest of the week."

"We'll have to keep thinking. I'll see you in the morning." His tone echoed her weariness. How could the mind absorb so much while the heart was almost numb with pain?

"Good night, Kevin."

Sophie watched him walk down the hall toward Carter's room. Caitlyn had put a twin bed in the boy's room when Carter had suffered with colic during the first few months of his life. She and Logan had taken turns tending to him in the middle of the night, allowing them to each get a good night's rest on alternating nights. Kevin had chosen to sleep there so Carter wouldn't wake up alone.

Sophie took her computer bag into Caitlyn's office and cleared a spot in the center of the desk to work on her clients' accounts, trying not to think about her dear friend. If she waited any longer to get started, she'd never catch up.

An hour later her mother arrived. Sophie let her in and went back to the desk.

Her mom followed her into the office. "You should be resting."

"I can't sleep." She closed one window on her computer screen and opened another to begin working on her next account. She needed to finish several more accounts before she could think about going to bed.

"I'm not surprised." She sat in the chair opposite the desk. "But if you don't rest, you'll exhaust yourself. Those kids will take a lot more out of you than you ever imagined would be possible. And you're grieving the loss of Caitlyn at the same time."

Sophie tapped the eraser of her pencil on her notepad. The nervous gesture was a habit, but a pencil was a vital tool for an accountant. At least that's what her favorite professor had said on her first day of college. "I know, Mom." Sophie looked up from her computer. "But I can't stop my mind from racing in a hundred different directions."

Caitlyn wasn't there to talk to anymore. Since they were kids, Sophie had turned to her best friend when she had a problem. As adults, more often than not, Caitlyn had been the one to convince Sophie to step away from work and remember to enjoy life. She'd miss her friend for the rest of her life. She wondered what Caitlyn's advice would be about tomorrow's court appearance.

"That's part of the grieving process. It'll ease in time, but grief won't be denied." Her mom ran her hand along the arms of the wooden chair and looked up. "Did you and Kevin come to a solution about tomorrow? I couldn't believe it when you called this afternoon and told me what Jackson said. Surely the judge won't expect you to give up the children just because you aren't married."

"We're going into court and asking for the will to be enforced like Logan and Caitlyn wrote it." She filled her mother in on the details she and Kevin had discussed. Repeating it didn't make it any less painful, and tomorrow they'd have to say it all to a judge. The continuous cycle of hard decisions, one after another, made her wonder if they'd ever have a chance to heal.

"That seems like a good plan, but what if the judge insists on a married couple? I don't know him, but his wife is a friend of mine. We've never talked about his work, but on occasion she's mentioned something that makes me think he's not one to be swayed once he's made up his mind."

Her mother hit at the core of everything that had crowded into her thoughts while she'd tried to work. Marriage to Kevin for the sake of the kids pounded in her mind over and over again. "I don't know." She dropped the pencil. "I might be willing to do it, but *only* for the kids. Kevin seems so set against it."

Her mother's eyes went wide and then relaxed so quickly that Sophie thought she imagined it. "He does?"

"He doesn't think it's right for the judge to insist." She huffed out a sigh. "You know our history. I'm the last person on earth Kevin Lane wants to marry."

"Your history was a long time ago." Her mother spoke in the measured tone she used when she was trying to stay neutral even though she had a strong opinion on a matter. "Maybe you're not being fair to him. Did you ask him what he thought about marrying for the kids?"

Sophie nodded. "He made it very plain when Jackson was here that he doesn't want to marry me."

"Did he say that? That he doesn't want to marry you?" Her mom pointed across the desk at her.

What kind of question was that? "He said he didn't want to marry. He didn't specify me, but that's a given."

"Don't be so sure that you know what Kevin is thinking about all of this. His life has been upended the same way yours has. And I seem to remember that you're the one who broke things off with Kevin. He didn't reject you."

"That was a long time ago, Mom. But, honestly, he's still that same adventurous free spirit he was then. You know I don't believe in taking unnecessary risks. Besides, we're both career-minded singles. Neither of us has dated for years." She'd never stopped to wonder why Kevin hadn't dated. She knew she'd never love anyone the way she'd loved him so she didn't put herself out there anymore. The pain of letting that love go had lasted too long. If she wasn't as happy in her soul as she had been as a teenager in love, who was? That kind of sweet abandonment of your heart to another person led to heartache.

"And why is that, Sophie? Maybe that's what you need to analyze instead of the numbers on that screen."

Sophie took in a deep breath. "I'm not going to talk about my single life tonight, Mom."

"Okay. We don't have to talk about it, but you need to think about it just the same." Her mother stood. "I'll be able to keep the kids during the day tomorrow, but I'm only off work for a few more days. I think the kids will adjust better if you implement your plans as quickly as possible."

"We agree. Thank you for all you've done." Sophie said another silent prayer that the judge would agree with their reasoning. The kids needed them. A new normal couldn't come soon enough. "I'm going to work for another hour or so, but you go on to bed."

"Don't work too late. Tomorrow is a big day. You don't want to go into court looking like you haven't slept."

"I'll be okay."

Her mother blew her a kiss. "Good night, Sophie. I'll be praying for you. And Kevin."

When her mom left, Sophie leaned back in the desk chair and rubbed her temples. The sofa in Caitlyn's office had served as a comfortable makeshift bed for her, but fatigue was the least of Sophie's problems.

Court, an inflexible judge, all the details for setting up the trust for the kids, dealing with everyone's new living arrangements… The list was endless, but court and the judge made the rest pale in comparison.

The last thing Sophie had time to think about was her mother's questions about why she never dated and her constant wish for Sophie to marry. It was a years-old argument that her mother insisted on having regularly.

She leaned her elbows on the desk and laced her fingers together.

Kevin hadn't specifically said he didn't want to marry her. But she'd hurt him terribly when she'd ended their relationship. Even if his heart had healed after all this time, it didn't seem possible that he'd ever want to marry her.

She knew one thing. He was still Kevin—the fearless man who refused to change.

The friendship they enjoyed now had grown out of being constantly thrown together by Logan and Caitlyn. Their best friends had insisted that they'd never attempt to set them up, and over time Kevin and Sophie had relaxed into an easy friendship. They all went to the same church, spent weekends together and loved those two kids.

Friendships could grow into deeper relationships, but

not with their history. At least she didn't think it could happen for them.

Tonight, she was learning the unknown was as stressful as grief.

God help us. Give Judge Carlisle the wisdom to know that Kevin and I need to raise Carter and Jade. We're the closest thing to parents those little ones have now.

Chapter Two

Kevin pulled at the knot in his tie. He'd never been to court before. Ever. But he knew that even if he'd been a hundred times, nothing would be more important than what was going to happen in the courtroom behind the heavy wooden doors he faced.

Sophie had told him a suit would be appropriate. Jackson had agreed.

Kevin regretted that conversation. If it hadn't happened minutes before he left the house this morning, he'd have figured out a way to talk them out of it. But he'd left Logan and Caitlyn's place early so he could go by his condo on the way to the courthouse.

In the wakeful hours of the night, he'd made the decision to come to court prepared for any possible scenario. He'd picked up something from his place just in case things didn't go the way he and Sophie planned. He patted his suit jacket to confirm that what he hoped was the last thing he might possibly need was still in his inside pocket.

"Stop fidgeting." Sophie slid her hand across his shoulders to smooth the back of his coat. He found the contact comforting. Although they were in this together—and separately—she was the only person who understood what he was going through because she was experiencing it at the same time.

He resorted to taunting her, hoping it would help distract him. "Seriously? That's all you've got for me?"

She lowered her hand to her side and shrugged. "It's all I have for me, too."

Jackson approached them. "Ten minutes, according to the bailiff. I'll see you both inside. We'll be at the table on the left in the front of the courtroom." He pulled the heavy door open and disappeared into the small, dark hall that served as a sound barrier between the courtroom and the rest of the courthouse.

Kevin took in a deep, calming breath and stared at the ceiling. He thought about praying, but he was all prayed out. If God didn't act on their behalf after all the begging he'd already done, there was no hope for them.

Sophie stood beside him, stiff and silent.

"It's going to be okay, Sophie." His words were more hopeful than true, but he had to say something.

"We don't know that." Her voice trembled. "None of this feels real. How can they be gone? Death is for the elderly and the sick, not for two young people so in love." She choked on the last words and tears flowed.

Kevin pulled her into his embrace and let her weep against his chest.

She didn't cry alone. Tears spilled onto his cheeks and dropped off his chin onto her thick, dark hair. Its fresh tropical scent helped to ease his pain.

Logan had been his best friend since the second grade. Kevin was about to take on the toughest role Logan had ever asked him to fill.

"You're right. It doesn't feel real. We've got to be strong, Sophie. Let's get through this hearing."

She pulled away from him and rubbed the tears from her face. She drew in a deep breath and blew it out again. "We can do this." She pivoted to stand beside him, and they faced the door again.

"We'll do it together." He took her hand in his. They'd borne so much over the last few days, it seemed natural to offer his physical support. They were friends now, though at one time they'd been so much more. He wouldn't let her suffer alone.

The courtroom door opened, and Jackson waved them in. "The judge is ready."

Kevin followed Jackson and Sophie into the courtroom and tried to steady his breathing. Today, everything about their future was on the line. He had to put the grief out of his mind and focus on the judge—a man who wasn't in the room.

Jackson led them through the swinging gate in the center of a low wall that separated the gallery from the people involved in the case at hand.

Dark wood-paneled walls and heavy furniture that was probably older than Kevin set a somber mood. He pulled out the middle chair for Sophie, then sat on her left. Jackson took the chair closest to the center of the room and leaned so he could see both of them.

"The judge took a recess after the last case. It was a tough one. I hope it doesn't affect us, but we need to be cautious. Sometimes the mood of one case can linger into the next." The tilt of the lawyer's head indicated concern to Kevin. "Are you two ready? A show of unity on every point is our best approach."

Kevin looked at Sophie. "Are we okay?"

She nodded. "Yes. I'm sorry for being so emotional."

Jackson picked up his pen and made a note on the legal pad in front of him. He must have caught the wariness in their exchange. "What is it?"

Sophie set her purse on the floor by her chair. "Nothing. We were just talking about how difficult all of this is. Our lives are changing so much."

A door in the back corner of the courtroom opened, and the bailiff called out for everyone to stand as the judge entered.

Jackson buttoned his suit coat as they stood. "We're about to find out just how much."

And with those words, Kevin's heart sank into his stomach.

The formalities of stating the case number and reading different aspects of their situation into the record droned on for the next five minutes. Five minutes that seemed like an eternity at first but actually served to settle Kevin's nerves.

Sophie sat quietly beside him, twisting her fingers together in her lap.

Judge Carlisle looked up from studying the papers in front of him. "Are all the parties present?"

Jackson stood. "Yes, Your Honor."

The judge took off his glasses and looked at Kevin and Sophie. Kevin's thoughts ran to what it must be like to stand in a criminal lineup. This man had powerful intimidation skills.

"I know there's a will to probate in this case, but let's start with the children. They are why I set the court date for today."

"Your Honor, as you've read, Logan and Caitlyn West chose Kevin Lane and Sophie Owens to be guardians for

Carter West and Jade West. Mr. Lane and Ms. Owens are here today to accept full responsibility for the minor children. They both served as godparents and had agreed to the choices that Mr. and Mrs. West made for their children. They have taken care of the children since the accident last week that took the lives of their parents."

The judge studied Kevin and Sophie while Jackson presented this information. "Is it the intention of your clients to separate the siblings?"

"No, Your Honor. Mr. Lane and Ms. Owens have known the children their entire lives. They were close friends of the parents and often socialized. They were actually tending to the children in the West family home the night Mr. and Mrs. West died."

"So, they have a history with the children." The judge picked up his pen and made a note.

"Yes, and Mr. Lane and Ms. Owens intend to raise the children in their parents' home."

Kevin didn't take his eyes off the judge. He wasn't sure he'd take another deep breath until the hearing was over.

Judge Carlisle looked up from his notes. "Mr. Lane and Ms. Owens will both reside in the home?"

Jackson cleared his throat. "Ms. Owens will reside in the home. Mr. Lane lives nearby and will assist Ms. Owens with the care of the children."

"That puts the children with only one full-time guardian, Mr. Yarbrough. It is rare for me to consider that arrangement to be in the best interest of the children."

Sophie's hand tightened on the arm of her chair, and Kevin captured it in his. He leaned close and whispered, "Wait. It's too early to panic."

She squeezed his fingers and held her breath.

"Your Honor, as godparents, Mr. Lane and Ms. Owens have built close relationships with the children and each other. Because neither of the West parents had living relatives, the godparents are the only other family the children have ever known."

Judge Carlisle tapped the bench with one finger. "But having a part-time father figure immediately after the loss of their parents would almost certainly harm them further. Placing them in a foster home with a married couple—much like the home they've known to date—would create a sense of security they'll need."

Kevin didn't like that the judge sounded as though he'd made his decision. Sophie must have sensed it, too, because she tightened her grip on his hand until the feeling started to leave his fingers.

Jackson shot a quick glance in their direction and turned back to the judge. "Both Mr. and Mrs. West were raised in foster care. They met in elementary school and grew close because of their circumstances. During her childhood, Mrs. West was placed in more than one bad situation. In one home, over the course of more than a year, she was subjected to physical punishment resulting in bruises that led to her removal from that home and a prison term for the former foster parent. She struggled with fear for the rest of her childhood."

Kevin appreciated Jackson's persistent fervor for their cause, but hearing Caitlyn's childhood pain summed up in a few sentences seemed inadequate given all she'd suffered. After everything she'd done as a mother to protect Jade and Carter, he didn't think he could bear it if the judge overrode her will.

Jackson paused, then continued in a measured tone, "Respectfully, Your Honor, she knew her situation was rare. Mr. West grew up in the system and had a text-book circumstance of everything done well. Even so, Mrs. West didn't want her children to ever be subjected to the possibility of foster care.

"It's why they were so diligent in choosing Mr. Lane and Ms. Owens. They were all close in school and continued their friendship into adulthood."

Their closeness had to count for something with Judge Carlisle. Kevin's gut twisted while he waited for the man who held Carter and Jade's future in his hands to speak.

The judge folded his arms across his chest and leaned back against his massive chair, the aged leather creaking with every movement. "Her case is unfortunate. I hate the rare occasion when situations like that arise and damage the reputation of a system put in place to help and protect children. I understand her reluctance, but I can't let an isolated incident that happened fifteen or twenty years ago keep me from doing the right thing for these children. I'm not willing to deny them what they need—and deserve. Two full-time guardians."

Judge Carlisle turned over a paper from one of the files in front of him. "In the foster care system, we have many qualified and proven married couples eager to serve children like this. As orphans, they'll be eligible for adoption. They are so young that it won't be difficult to find them a permanent home where they'll be raised in a complete family unit. Not with someone popping in and out of their lives when Mr. Lane decides he has time to visit."

Kevin leaned forward in his chair and cleared his throat. How could a judge who didn't even know him make such a negative assumption? It wasn't right, and he wouldn't sit by and let it happen. He started to stand, but Sophie tugged on his arm as Jackson held out a hand, keeping him in his seat.

Jackson tried to persuade the judge to hear him out. "Your Honor, I assure you Mr. Lane has every intention of being a full-time guardian. I am confident Mr. Lane and Ms. Owens could legally adopt the children. They're more than willing to do whatever it takes to provide a good and loving home for these children—to fulfill the promises they made to their parents."

Jackson paused and gestured toward Kevin and Sophie. "Mr. and Mrs. West knew Mr. Lane and Ms. Owens. They were dear friends, chosen out of love and concern for their children's future. I daresay, with more concern than most parents because Mrs. West knew the risks of not preparing properly for them."

The judge wasn't swayed by Jackson's argument. "The best interest of the children carries more weight than a friendship with their parents. In my years on the bench, I've found stability after such a traumatic loss is vital to a child's future. I want to place them in a home with two parents."

Kevin felt as if the judge were physically ripping Jade and Carter away from him. He couldn't listen quietly to where this was going. "Your Honor—"

Jackson held his hand out to warn Kevin to be quiet, but the children needed someone to defend them—to fight for them. And Jackson, though an excellent lawyer, didn't have a stake in the future of the kids.

Kevin stood. "No, Jackson. I want to be heard."

The judge waved off Jackson's objection. "I'm listening, Mr. Lane."

Kevin wasn't sure if Judge Carlisle's serious tone bode well for the outcome, but he had to say something.

"Your Honor, there are two of us." He pointed at Sophie and then himself.

"But you aren't together. A stable home is key for children. They've lost so much."

"We are together." Kevin looked at Sophie and tried to read her thoughts. He hoped she would understand his desperation and agree.

Bewilderment. That's what he saw in her face.

"What are you saying, Kevin?" Her voice was barely more than a whisper.

"What are you saying, young man?" Judge Carlisle seemed on the verge of losing his patience.

Kevin gulped and leaned close to Sophie. He'd prepared for every possibility, and had prayed it wouldn't happen this way. "I need to talk to you. Privately." He gave a nod in the direction of the small hallway outside the courtroom doors, but it was obvious she didn't follow his intent.

"Mr. Lane, I must insist that you address the bench. I've been generous to allow you this time, but I have a full docket today. I need to know what you mean when you say you and Ms. Owens are together."

Kevin ignored the judge. He had to convince Sophie to hear him out. "Please. It's important."

Confusion filled her gaze, but she nodded. "Okay."

Kevin caught Jackson's eye over the top of Sophie's head. "Can you get us fifteen minutes?" Though he'd have to talk fast to convince her to go along with his plan in such a short time, he'd give it his all.

Jackson shrugged. "Your Honor, we'd like to ask the

court's indulgence for a brief recess. My clients want to clarify a point in the case before we proceed."

"I'm not here at your leisure, Mr. Yarbrough." Judge Carlisle frowned again. "But given the serious nature of this case, I'll make an exception. You may use the adjoining conference room in the back corner. If you leave the courtroom, I'll call in the social worker and place the children somewhere today. They don't deserve to be unsettled for a minute beyond what is necessary." He picked up his gavel and rapped it on the bench.

"Court is in recess for fifteen minutes." He used the gavel to point at Kevin. "Not a minute more."

"Thank you, Your Honor." Kevin knew this was his only shot at maintaining guardianship of the kids. He couldn't blow it.

The judge stood, and the bailiff called for everyone to rise.

As soon as the judge went through a door that led to his chambers, Kevin took Sophie by the arm and directed her toward the conference room.

He prayed she'd hear him out and agree, so they could keep those sweet kids.

If anyone in the world loved Jade and Carter as much as he did, it was Sophie. She'd already given up so much for them. Would she risk a future tied to him if that's what it took to seal the deal?

She isn't a risk taker.

Kevin pushed that thought out of his mind.

He never imagined he'd propose to Sophie in a courthouse conference room. He hoped it was the right thing to do.

The boisterous beating of his heart settled as he ushered her into the small room, and a bravery stronger than any he'd ever felt settled over him. He was about to take the biggest risk of his life.

Sophie pivoted to confront Kevin the instant he closed the door. "What were you thinking? We can't upset the judge. He holds all the power in this situation. And it looks like we're losing." She knew Kevin would never intentionally put the outcome of the hearing in jeopardy, yet that was what he was doing by interrupting the proceedings. She hoped he hadn't done irreparable damage.

He clawed his hands through his coarse hair. "I know, but I couldn't just sit there and listen to him give Jade and Carter to strangers. We have to do something."

Sophie felt as helpless as he sounded. "What can we do? We came in here with a united front to tell him that we want to do everything according to the will, but Judge Carlisle doesn't seem to be listening to Jackson."

"Jackson is a very good attorney, but his hands are tied. He can't make the judge listen to our side."

"And he warned us this could happen." Sophie slumped into a chair at the small conference table. "I feel so powerless." She fumbled with the chain around her neck that held her father's wedding ring. She always wore it on important occasions. She couldn't imagine a more important day than today. It helped to think that the part of her that was her father might rise up to meet any challenge and win. He was the bravest man she'd ever known.

Kevin paced the floor in the tiny room. A room made tinier by the fervor of his motion. His spontaneity was on full display today. The part of him that took risks and left her feeling vulnerable and endangered could cost them guardianship of the children—and cost the children the lives their parents had chosen for them. There was more at stake here than a thrill ride on white water or a climb up a steep mountain. Lives hung in the balance. And his actions didn't just affect him. She could pay the price for his recklessness today.

In an instant he stopped and dropped into the chair beside her. "Let's get married."

Sophie's head was spinning. "You can't be serious. We talked about this. You didn't want to consider marriage at all." The stress must be hitting him harder than she'd realized.

"I know, but honestly, I couldn't sleep last night. I know I said it was ridiculous. Now, I don't think we have a choice. Not in Judge Carlisle's court. Even though I came here hoping it would go the way Logan and Caitlyn intended, something in my gut kept forcing me to consider Jackson's warnings about marriage. I've thought about it in every imaginable way."

"So have I." Sleep had evaded her until the early morning hours when fatigue had carried her into a restless slumber. "But marriage? You and me? No. I think you were right. It's not a good idea." She looked at her watch. "We only have ten minutes left." Ten minutes would never be long enough to overcome her fear of his dangerous ways. Ten years hadn't been long enough.

He leaned one elbow on the table and turned toward her. "Think about it. All marriages used to be arranged."

"This is not the Wild West, where a mail-order bride gets off the train and marries the man who bought her ticket."

"No. We're a much more informed society, but really—how many romantic marriages fail?"

For some reason she couldn't define, she knew he wanted an answer. "I don't know. Half?"

"Yes." He stood again and paced. The pacing must be his way to vent the stress that threatened to overwhelm them. "Is there anyone in your world you think you could love forever in a romantic marriage?"

She immediately knew her answer, even if she didn't dare to speak it. At one time, Kevin had been the person she'd imagined spending her forever with. She'd loved him as much as she'd known how to love anyone at eighteen.

But he'd put his fun ahead of her. Losing her dad in a motorcycle accident had taken the bravado out of her. She saw danger everywhere after that day.

Kevin was a self-proclaimed adventurer. He spent his life going from one thrill to the next. She hadn't been brave enough to live like that anymore, and he hadn't been willing to change.

She answered him honestly. "No. There's no one." The one she'd wanted romance with had chosen a life she could never embrace.

Kevin came to stand by her chair and went down on one knee. He reached for her hand. "Sophie Owens, will you marry me?"

"Kevin, we're almost out of time."

"I know. Hear me out." He held her hand in his. "No one knows we aren't a couple. No one in the court system anyway. We were always spending time together with Logan and Caitlyn." They both grimaced at the fact that those special times were over.

He didn't let the sorrow stop him from making his

point. "We can marry and move into the house. It's big enough for separate rooms and an office for your accounting business. You can be home with the kids while I work at the sporting goods store. I can take care of them in the evenings to give you time to work."

"It's so much to think about, Kevin. What about you? Don't you want to marry for love?"

His face broke into a grin. "You know I'm too carefree to build a relationship, much less fall in love."

She didn't want to believe that. Still, he'd never shown any interest in a long-term relationship with anyone. They'd both dated other people on and off through the last ten years, but neither of them had ever been serious with anyone after their high school courtship. "I guess neither of us is any good at romance."

"It's not like you or I were ever going to marry for real. We can do this, Sophie. We're friends." He smiled up at her. "We've always been together with the kids. They don't have anyone without us. It's the last thing we can do for Logan and Caitlyn. We promised when we stood in the church the day the kids were dedicated."

"I can still hear Caitlyn's voice when she asked if you'd marry me if you had to." Sophie sniffed to keep from crying. "She was being her funny self." Caitlyn had made the teasing remark, and they'd all laughed when Kevin put a hand across his heart and promised to do his duty if ever he was called upon. Sophie had accepted his offered hand at the time and bowed her head in agreement like a heroine in a Shakespearean play.

"But we agreed. At least I did. I seem to remember that you didn't object." He gave her a sad smile. "I'll admit that I never imagined it happening. At the time it was a hypothetical situation that made us all laugh and none of us thought possible."

"Yet here we are." It was surreal to her, and at the same time, it was very real. "My vows at the dedication meant something."

"Mine, too." He chuckled. "It's like the verse in Psalm 15 that says God honors someone who keeps their vow even if it hurts."

"There is pain in this situation, but at least we know we're not the kind to hurt one another." She cringed inwardly at the memory of the pain in his face when she'd broken off their relationship. "Not anymore." It wouldn't be fair to him not to acknowledge that she'd hurt him in the past.

"No. Good friends don't." His matter-of-fact tone was sober.

"I know I hurt you in the past—"

Kevin held up his hand to stop her. "We were young. Young people do and say things. We're far beyond that."

"It was a long time ago." She remembered the pain she'd endured, too. "Kevin, there's something you need to know about me. I mean, really know and understand."

He raised his brows and waited.

Sophie hated exposing her deepest thoughts to him, but if they were going to even consider getting married, she'd have to go into the relationship with him knowing her true feelings. Anything less would be dishonest. "I'm not bold like you. Life has taught me to be cautious. It's a fundamental difference between us. You're a risk taker. I'm not. Everything that scared me all those years ago—when we broke up—still scares me."

Compassion filled his eyes. "You have to face your fears to conquer them, Sophie." He gave her hand a slight squeeze. "I've heard parenting isn't for wimps. We're both doing this. By joining forces, I think we can give Jade and Carter a better life. You just have to be willing to take a leap of faith with me."

"I can't ride zip lines or climb rock walls, Kevin."

"I won't ask you to." When she cringed, he added, "And I promise to be careful."

Sophie knew that was probably the most he would promise. He was who he was. "I still don't like it."

"Don't worry." He winked. "Parenthood and marriage are the scariest things I've ever tried to do."

"I'm serious, Kevin. It's too quick. And I don't think the judge will believe us. As much as I know we have to figure something out for the sake of the kids, it's just too rash." Kevin pulled his strong fingers across the muscles in the back on his neck as if he hoped to knead away the tension. He was upset with her caution. She could see it on his face. Then he exhaled and grasped her hands.

"If you won't marry me, will you accept my proposal for an engagement? Even a temporary engagement, just until the judge retires? That will show him—and anyone else who asks—that we're in a committed relationship. Only you and I need to know it's a commitment to the kids and not each other."

She glanced at the sweeping second hand on the wall clock that ticked away their precious time, and the pressure in her head pounded. With a deep breath, she got to the heart of the matter. "It's easy for you to throw out proposals. Your life is a journey from one emotional high to the next. To me, marriage *and* engagement are commitments. Lifelong commitments. Whether they're exciting or not."

He flinched. She knew her words wounded him, but if there was ever a time for complete honesty, this was it.

"I'm a grown man now, Sophie. I made a lifelong commitment when I became a godparent. You know I've honored that vow, because we've done it together." He released her hands. "I'm not asking you to fall in love with me again. I'm asking you to join forces with me to keep this judge from taking away any hope we have of keeping those kids and raising them together." He tilted his head to one side and looked into her eyes, deep into her soul like no one else had ever been able to do. "Can you do that with me? As friends?"

Her resolve started to crumble. Really, they'd already promised to work together for the kids. Had that pledge bound them together as a family? Reading bedtime stories and doing life together might be more of a commitment than most truly engaged couples realized.

"As friends?" She swallowed her fear. "I suppose it could work. We've already committed to sharing our lives with the kids. If anyone asks about a wedding, we tell them we're focusing on the kids for the foreseeable future?"

"Sounds good to me."

Shyness filled her for a quick instant. "Are you sure about all of this?" Was she considering a fake engagement to Kevin? This conversation would never have happened a week ago.

He looked more serious than she'd ever seen him. "What is love to you?"

Not the question she expected. "Caring for someone besides yourself. Putting the needs of someone else above your own desires."

He nodded. "To me, love is commitment. I can commit to you, Sophie. To our new family. Can you?"

Something inside her melted. She had prayed for God to have His hand in the events of the day. This was not one of the ways she'd expected Him to answer.

A sudden peace that she could commit to Kevin and the children gave her the courage to say her next words. "I can. Until the guardianship is finalized." She nodded and smiled. "As friends."

"As friends." He released her hands and they both stood. "Okay, then."

She hummed a sigh and nodded. "Okay." She'd just made what could be the biggest decision of her life in a ten-minute window of time. A lot could go wrong if the judge discovered their open-ended agreement to eventually dissolve the engagement.

Sure, she'd thought about endless possible scenarios nonstop since Jackson came to the house yesterday, but in the grand scheme of life, that was no time at all. She prayed it was the right choice.

The only man she'd ever wanted to marry had just proposed to her. And she'd said yes. Without the fanfare of romance and roses, she'd agreed to an engagement of commitment and friendship.

Not unlike the way she orchestrated the rest of her life. On the surface, she should be happy to have the matter settled. Only the two of them would know they'd never marry.

Inside she ignored the heaviness of her soul as it wept over dreams that died with her decision. There would be no romance for her. By the time the kids were grown, and she and Kevin went their separate ways, her time for romance would be long past.

Even after the judge retired and the engagement ended, she didn't think anyone would want a relationship with her while she raised two kids with Kevin.

In her heart she knew her hope for love with the man of her dreams had died ten years ago when Kevin hadn't accepted that her fear of losing him in an accident had become a permanent part of her.

And lose him, she did.

Now she had him back—in name only. And only for the kids.

She still worried. "What if the judge finds out this engagement isn't real? Or our friends? Will someone tell him? Gran Colina is a small town." Terror struck her heart. "We could lose Jade and Carter forever."

Kevin slid his fingers into the inside pocket of his jacket. "Relax. It is real." He pulled out an engagement ring. Why did he have a ring? Where did he get it? And when? She was dumbfounded into silence as he slid it onto her finger. "We are truly committed to this relationship. As a family. That's real. And if we have problems with the engagement, they won't be for long. The judge's term is only for two more years."

His words frightened Sophie more. Would he abandon his commitment then? She shook her head. No, he'd keep his word. For the kids. And he hadn't really promised her anything except friendship.

Kevin was a risk taker, but he was always honest.

Still, he'd given himself an out by mentioning the judge's term. Grief clouded her mind. It was impossible to process a temporary engagement, guardianship and make major life decisions with the one man on earth who had the power to rattle her thinking.

She opened her mouth to ask him to clarify, but there

was a knock at the door, and Jackson opened it. "Two minutes. Did you come to a conclusion? I need you to tell me before we go back in."

Kevin put his arm around Sophie's shoulders. "We know what we're going to do."

"And?" Jackson looked over his shoulder into the courtroom. "Too late. The bailiff is waving us in."

"It's going to be all right." Kevin clapped Jackson on the shoulder as they took their places behind the table. Sophie glimpsed Jackson's concerned expression and wished they'd had time to explain to him.

Judge Carlisle banged the gavel and told everyone to take a seat.

"Except for you, Mr. Lane. I want you to answer my question. What do you mean when you say you and Ms. Owens are together?"

Kevin rested his hand on her shoulder, and she realized she was trembling. "We're engaged."

Jackson jerked his head to stare at Kevin. If the moment wasn't so serious, Sophie would be tempted to laugh. She permitted herself a small smile. If she hadn't, there was a strong possibility that she might burst into tears. Her emotions were all over the place. Like all the bad jokes she'd ever heard about pregnancy hormones.

In a way, that made sense to her. She and Kevin were at a moment of transition that would bring them and two young children together as a family. If the judge agreed.

"Mr. Lane, this court will not tolerate falsehood in any fashion."

"It's not false, Your Honor. Sophie and I—Ms. Owens—made a promise to Logan and Caitlyn in church on the day they dedicated their children. Caitlyn asked us to marry in the event the children were ever orphaned, and we agreed. So, in a way, we've been engaged for a year."

"Is this a ploy to gain guardianship of the children and later dissolve your so-called engagement?"

"Our commitment to each other and the children is lifelong." Kevin squeezed her shoulder. Pride at how he stood his ground made her reach up and cover his hand with hers.

"Mr. Yarbrough, were you aware of this?"

Jackson tugged at his collar. "We did talk about it for a brief moment yesterday after the funeral for the Wests. We didn't get into the details, but Mr. Lane is telling you the truth about their conversation with Mrs. West at the dedication. I was in attendance for the event."

Judge Carlisle lifted a copy of the will and read for a few moments. "Ms. Owens, is all that's been said here today true?"

Sophie stood and slipped her hand into Kevin's for moral support. "Yes, Your Honor, it is."

"I'm not inclined to accept this. It seems a bit too convenient to me. You can't just up and promise to marry without considering the long-term changes it will make in your lives. These children will be in a home for the next seventeen or eighteen years. Marriage is for a lifetime." He shook his head. "If it's not a good marriage, it stands to do more harm than good to the children. Your friendship with their parents, and even your friendship with one another, isn't enough to satisfy the court that your relationship will last."

Sophie could see Judge Carlisle setting his mind against them. There was nothing to do but confront him with the truth.

"Your Honor, if I may, your wife is a friend of my mother's."

He held up a hand to stop her from speaking. "That won't sway me."

She pressed her hand over her heart. "No, sir, I wouldn't suggest such a thing." She cleared her throat. "What I'm saying is, didn't you marry your wife soon after her first husband died overseas?"

The judge leaned against the tufted leather of his chair and crossed his arms. "I did."

"And didn't she have kids?"

"Three."

Jackson sank into his chair. The poor guy didn't seem to know how to help her and Kevin.

"Weren't you her husband's best friend?"

Judge Carlisle sat in silence for a long moment. He tapped his finger against the papers on his bench.

"Ordinarily, people don't come into my courtroom and ask me questions, Ms. Owens."

Sophie's heart sank. She'd hoped he'd see how she and Kevin were trying to do the same thing he'd done, but Jackson had warned them that he held a tight rein on his court. Words failed her. In a matter of hours, they could be packing suitcases for Jade and Carter to move in with someone who would become their new parents. Someone they didn't know. And all hope could be lost.

She made one final plea. "I'm only saying that, like Logan and Caitlyn, none of us has a guarantee. All we can do is pray and do our best. Kevin and I have committed to each other and pledge to do our best for the children. In a way, it's like what you and your wife did."

Jackson stood again. "Your Honor, I'm sure the grief of my clients and their love for the West children have motivated their actions today. Please know they meant no disrespect to the court."

The judge shook his head. "I recognize the motivations at play here, Counselor." He leaned his elbows on the bench and steepled his fingers.

"Mr. Lane and Ms. Owens, I need more than your assertion that your engagement isn't an arrangement intended to win your case today."

Sophie looked into Kevin's eyes and then back to the judge. "Your Honor, we made this commitment when we agreed to be godparents. It came after a lot of prayer and consideration. Logan and Caitlyn were adamant that we be willing to do whatever it took to raise these kids. When we made the pledge to them, before God and His church, we made it to each other, too."

Kevin tightened his hold on her hand. She knew he shared the depth of her desperation.

"Is this how you feel, Mr. Lane?"

"It is, Your Honor."

"Okay, then." Judge Carlisle made a note on the paper in front of him. "The court will order a home inspection and schedule a hearing in four weeks to follow up on this case."

He narrowed his gaze on Kevin and Sophie. "If I find out that this engagement isn't real, I'll act accordingly." He picked up the gavel. "I think we're done for the morning then."

Sophie exhaled a slow breath as the judge left the courtroom.

There would be things to work through, but she and Kevin would manage them together like Kevin had said. She'd just faced her fear of losing the kids. No zip line, rope bridge—or even skydiving—could terrify her more.

She'd think about Kevin's adventurous nature later. Surely, he'd realize that, as a parent, certain changes in his lifestyle would need to be made. For now, though, he'd proved his commitment to his new role beyond question.

Today, they'd come together to ensure Jade and Carter would be sleeping in their own beds tonight. And, hopefully, every night for the rest of their childhoods.

Chapter Three

Sophie's mind was in a spin as she drove to Logan and Caitlyn's house after she and Kevin left the courthouse. They'd driven separately that morning because Kevin had said he needed to run an errand on the way to court. She was glad of the privacy now. Deep breathing wasn't enough to restore her calm. Prayer—out loud, in the car, alone—helped.

Their temporary engagement had secured the kids' future. Sophie hoped and prayed that was true.

Judge Carlisle had signed off on the guardianship pending an investigation by a social worker from the county department for child protection services. Jackson had assured her and Kevin that it was a routine matter. He saw no problems in the near or distant future for their new family.

Family.

Last week she'd been a single woman, independent and focused on her career. Today she was a mother—with a fiancé. Sort of.

Her fingers tightened on the steering wheel, and she stared at the ring on her left hand. Becoming Jade and

Carter's guardian had sent her life reeling out of control last week. Today, the reeling stopped with a suddenness that jerked her into a new reality, one she was even more unprepared for.

Someone in the car behind her tapped their horn. She didn't know how long she'd been sitting at the green light, but she took her foot off the brake and slowly made the last turn before arriving at the house. She'd have to explain everything to her mother.

She parked behind Kevin's pickup. On autopilot she grabbed the paperwork that proved all the life changes were real and got out of her car.

Kevin climbed out of his truck and closed the door. "You look like I feel."

"Thanks." She had no energy for more than the one syllable. "I'm wondering how to tell my mother."

"Did she know the judge might insist on a married couple?"

"Yes, but I told her we were going to insist that the will be enforced as written." She looked up into his brown eyes. "I'm not sure how we should handle this *engagement*. It's every mother's dream for her daughter to marry and have a family. What will she think?"

He shoved his hands into the pockets of his suit pants. The jacket hung over one arm. He'd never been a man to wear business attire. The uniform for Adventure Lane Sports looked more like an outfit for a man on safari and suited him to perfection. "Tell her the truth. It's real. For now. Just like we agreed."

Was it? She didn't think so. At least it wouldn't be after Judge Carlisle retired.

Her mind jumped from one random thought to another. She hated the disorder of it, but there was one thing she needed to know. "Where did you get a ring? I don't need anything so fancy. This is too expensive." It didn't seem right that he'd purchased something so extravagant.

A shadow crossed his dark eyes so quickly that she blinked, unsure she'd really seen it. "Keep it."

She held up her left hand for him to see it. "This is why you wanted to drive separately today." The beauty of the ring made her want to keep it, but it wasn't right. Not under the circumstances. "I'm sure you can get your money back."

He looked away. "It doesn't matter." He was hiding something.

"It matters to me." Sophie grabbed his arm with her ringed hand. "Please talk to me."

"I'll tell you that I didn't go out and buy it this morning, so you don't have to worry about the cost." He backed away from her and loosened his tie. "I need to change clothes."

"Sure." Pressing him wouldn't make him tell her more. She knew him that well.

The front door opened as they walked up the sidewalk, and Jade came onto the porch. "Soapy! I missed you." The little girl's light blond hair lifted in the breeze. "Hi, K. We're eating grilled cheese for lunch. Miss Diane promised."

Kevin tapped the end of her nose. "Grilled cheese is my favorite. Can I have one, too?"

"Say please." Jade giggled and took his hand.

The look Kevin gave Sophie masked any thoughts she hoped to read in his eyes. "I'll take over with the kids and give you and your mother a few minutes to talk."

Sophie followed the two of them into the house. Her mother stood just inside the entrance.

"What is it?" Her mother's face filled with concern.

"Everything is fine. There are some details I need to tell you. Let's go into the office so we can talk privately." Sophie led the way to the room and dropped her purse and the paperwork onto the desk.

Her mother gasped. "You're engaged?" She grabbed Sophie's hand and studied the ring.

"I should have known you'd see that before I had a chance to explain. Let's sit and talk."

"Did he propose before or after court?" An innate excitement that Sophie suspected all moms were gifted with when it came to their daughter's marriages filled her mother's voice.

"During." Sophie sat next to her mom on the sofa.

"What?" Her confused face almost made Sophie laugh.

"If you'll take a breath, I'll explain everything."

"I can't believe you're engaged. You decided years ago that you and Kevin weren't meant for each other." Her mom put a hand to her lips. "I'm sorry. I shouldn't bring up the past at a time like this." The initial excitement turned to deep concern. "Are you sure you should marry him? It's not as if you're in love."

"Mom. Please." Sophie took a deep breath. The difficulty of this conversation increased with every phrase her mother uttered. "Relax. We're engaged, not married. And it all happened so fast."

"But engagement is the last step before marriage."

Sophie walked an emotional tightrope of truth. She loved her mother and would never mislead her. "Yes,

Kevin and I are engaged." She took a breath. "But right now, our focus is on the kids. Not ourselves."

All the color drained from her mom's face.

"Are you okay, Mom?"

Her mother leaned into the corner of the sofa. "Are you actually going to *marry* Kevin for the kids?"

Why did everything in the last week come with shock and lifelong consequences? Would the choices and changes slow down or continue at this chaotic pace? "It's complicated."

That was an understatement. Probably because her mind couldn't process everything in one moment. The trickling out of the facts was as much for her own benefit as for her mom's.

"Why? What?" Her mom appeared stunned.

"The judge was going to take the children away from us. Today. True to Jackson's word, the man insisted on a couple to care for the children." Sophie gave her mother a condensed version of the morning's events.

"But is this the right thing for you and Kevin? Engagement? It's a big commitment. Not as permanent as marriage, but from what you said about this Judge Carlisle, it may as well be."

"That's exactly what Kevin said." Sophie shrugged. Like most young women, Sophie had dreamed of love and romance. Not anymore. "And that's what we agreed to. A commitment to make a family for the children."

If she was honest with herself, it would have been more difficult—impossible—to accept a proposal from Kevin if it had been for any reason other than commitment to the children on mutually agreed to, friendly terms. Not being emotionally attached to him might take away some of the fear she'd felt over his safety all those years before. All she really had was his promise to be careful.

"Oh, baby." Her mother patted Sophie's cheek. "I just want you to be happy."

She wanted that, too. For all of them. All she could do was look at the positives and hope for the best. Her accountant tendencies took over, and she listed off the things she'd have written in a pros and cons spreadsheet if she'd had the time in that conference room. "He's a good Christian man. We both prayed before we went to court. There was no other choice. The kids need us."

"I know he's a good man. I'm just surprised. More than I would have been if this had happened before you went to college. In the years since then, you've seemed determined *not* to be in a relationship with Kevin."

Sophie hugged her mom. "Sometimes life changes faster than we expect. I promise you that Kevin and I are committed to make this work. For the sake of the kids." Saying it out loud reaffirmed the truth. Jade and Carter were the reason she and Kevin were going to such extraordinary lengths to satisfy the judge. And they were worth it.

"But are you committed to each other?" Doubt rang in her mother's voice. Sophie had heard it too many times to mistake it. It was the tone she'd used when Sophie had broken off her relationship with Kevin in their youth, and again when she'd refused an offer after graduation from college to work for a big accounting firm in Dallas for more money than she'd ever make in Gran Colina. She'd made the choice to be near her mother, and she'd never been sorry. There were things money couldn't buy.

Yes, she was committed to building a family for Jade and Carter. With Kevin. "We are." She forced a smile.

Her mom would have to be satisfied with that. Sophie needed to convince herself before she could convince anyone else.

Her mother didn't need to know that Kevin's commitment to the kids was lifelong, but the commitment he'd made to Sophie would expire when the judge retired.

No one needed to know that.

She smiled for her mother's sake, trying to put everything in the best possible light. "Everything will work out. We just need time to sort out the details."

Her mother stood as if to leave, then turned and said, "You know that's the ring he bought for you before you left for college."

Sophie jerked her hand up to look at the ring. "What?" Kevin had bought her a ring? They'd been so young. She'd hoped to marry him but didn't expect him to propose until she finished college.

"He asked your dad for permission to marry you before your birthday in your senior year." Her mom smiled at the memory. "Your dad gave his permission but asked him to wait until after graduation and made Kevin promise it would be a long engagement. He showed us the ring then. He was going to ask you the night before you left town." Sadness flashed across her mother's face. "Before everything else happened." They didn't need to say the words to know her mother referred to her father's death.

She couldn't think about her dad right now. He'd wanted to be at her wedding. They'd practiced their father-daughter dance since she was a little girl. No. That was a memory for another day. Now she was engaged with no wedding in sight.

Something in her heart crumbled to learn that she was engaged to the one man her father had approved.

Only she hadn't approved of Kevin then. She'd rejected him because he was so like the father she'd lost in an unnecessary accident.

Why had her mother never told her? "How can you be sure it's the same ring?"

"It's inscribed." Her mom was almost flippant, like Sophie should have known this. "Didn't he ever tell you?"

"No." Sophie tugged off the ring and looked for whatever message Kevin had chosen all those years ago for her to remember for the rest of their lives. "There's nothing here." She didn't know if she was relieved or sad.

"Oh, I'm sorry. The inscription was on the wedding band."

Had he brought the wedding band with him to court? Had he been willing to marry her if it had come to that? Even if he had kept the rings from another time in their lives, it was impossible that he still considered the sentiments to hold true.

She slid the ring back onto her finger. What would her life have been like if they hadn't ended their relationship years ago?

That wasn't fair. *She* had ended it. Would they be married with their own kids? Or would their differences have driven them apart in the end?

They weren't the same people they had been then. Not anymore.

They were friends now. And parents.

Kevin flipped the last grilled cheese sandwich onto a plate. "These are the best sandwiches ever. All we need to add is apple slices."

He kept one eye on the office door while he prepared

lunch. He hoped Diane would understand why he had proposed to Sophie. They'd have enough to handle in this new arrangement without being at odds with Sophie's mom.

"I want fish." Jade climbed onto a stool at the island. It still made him nervous to watch her do it, but she was nimble. The adventurer in him admired her skill.

"Apples for lunch." He poured milk into their cups, secured the lids and put a plate in front of each child. "Fish crackers will be a fun snack later." They held hands and gave thanks.

The office door opened, and Sophie and Diane joined them. He tensed again, as if he still stood before Judge Carlisle. The judge had held power over the kids, and—as a surrogate grandmother to the children—Diane would be a part of his life from now on.

Sophie tickled Jade as she walked by her stool on the way to the refrigerator. "This looks yummy, Jade. Did you cook while I was talking to Miss Diane?"

"You're silly, Soapy."

Kevin and her mom laughed with Jade. The laughter didn't alleviate the tightness in his gut.

Diane sat at the island with the kids and stared at him.

He wanted to squirm inside his skin. "So, did you hear our news?"

"I did." She picked up a slice of apple. "Not what I was expecting."

Kevin didn't know if her demeanor was a good or bad thing. "Life's surprises. I've lived my life seeking out new adventures—I didn't expect my biggest one to come like this."

"I'm not sure it's the wisest choice for the two of you." Diane's shoulders lifted on a sigh. "Given your history."

Sophie closed the refrigerator door and handed her mom a bottle of water, then sat at the island. "Mom, I told you the judge insisted."

Kevin understood Diane's complaint. "He actually said that if we left the courtroom he'd call for a social worker and arrange placement today." He chose his words carefully so Jade wouldn't ask questions. Sometimes he thought she was three going on thirteen. Even when he thought she was occupied with a toy or video, she'd surprise him and latch onto something he said.

"Well, Sophie told me about your *commitment*." Diane twisted the cap off her water bottle. "I trust you'll honor the promises you made to her father when you asked his permission to marry her."

Kevin thought the knot in his gut was tough until pain jolted through him at Diane's words. He pivoted to see Sophie's reaction.

She knew. He saw the pain and confusion in her eyes.

He would never have told her about his conversation with her dad, and he wished Diane hadn't. Now he'd have to explain.

I'm sorry. He mouthed the words so only Sophie could see.

She gave a curt nod and picked up half of her sandwich. "Thanks for making lunch."

"You're welcome." He forced his words to sound normal.

The challenges of this day just kept coming.

"Diane, Sophie and I haven't had time to process everything that's happened. I can assure you that I'll honor my promises to her—" he tried to catch Sophie's gaze, but she stared at her plate "—and to her father."

Sophie's gasp was quick and quiet. He didn't think her mother even heard it.

"That's good to hear." Diane tore Carter's sandwich into tiny bits and caught his milk cup when he knocked it over on the tray of the high chair. "You're sure right about life's surprises. I'd say you're both in for an adventure with this new family you have here." She turned her attention over to Jade.

When he sat down to eat his sandwich, Sophie looked up. Words she didn't say danced in her eyes. Probably a rebuke about the danger of adventure. It wouldn't be the first time. When Diane quoted back his statement about life's surprises and adventure, he decided he should have chosen his words with more care.

Adventure was the reason Sophie had broken things off with him the summer after she'd graduated. Only three weeks before he'd been planning to propose to her. He'd wanted to start his junior year at college knowing he'd be working for more than just a business degree. He'd wanted to build a life with her.

She'd rejected him, not for another person, but for no one. She'd rejected his character and called him selfish and irresponsible after a zip-lining accident that, rather than being fatal, had left him with only a broken collarbone and a few stitches because of the safety equipment he'd used.

Carter coughed and sputtered, drawing Kevin's mind back to the moment. He wiped a dribble of milk from the child's chin. "Slow down, big guy. We've got plenty of milk. No need to guzzle."

Carter held his cup by one handle and banged it on the tray of the high chair. Milk shot out of the holes in the top of the cup, making him laugh from his belly.

"Oh, no you don't." Kevin took the cup from him and offered a bite of the sandwich. "Have some of this." He wiped up the milk and accepted this new facet of his life again. Last week any spill he had to clean up would have been his own. Now he was responsible for everything to do with this tiny human.

And his sister. And, to a certain extent, Sophie.

Every moment seemed to hold a new challenge.

As soon as they finished the meal, it was time for both kids to go down for a nap. Sophie put Jade to bed, while Kevin took care of Carter. Diane had left to run some errands, and Kevin went into the office to find Sophie.

She sat behind the desk, staring out of the large window that overlooked the backyard. He settled on the sofa, and they sat in silence for a long time.

How did you start a conversation with a fiancée you knew didn't want to be engaged to you? His *fiancée* was the woman who'd turned him off the idea of ever marrying anyone. Where did they begin?

Sophie solved the problem for him by speaking first. "Thank you, Kevin." She still stared out into the yard.

"For what?"

"Doing what had to be done. Taking the initiative." She turned to him then and held up her left hand. "Mom told me about the ring."

"What about it?" It was as beautiful as he'd imagined on her slender hand. The sparkle of the diamond in the afternoon sun that streamed in through the office window was brilliant. He'd known it would be perfect for her when he'd seen it in the showcase at the jewelry store. The irony of her wearing it—without the love he'd intended to promise with it—stung.

"She told me that you showed them the ring when you talked to my dad."

"I'm surprised she remembered." He hoped Diane hadn't told Sophie about the wedding band, too.

Sophie caught his gaze and held it. "I never knew."

He waved off her words. "It was a long time ago." It was hard enough to be engaged to her, however temporary, knowing she hadn't wanted him when he'd loved her with all of his heart. He'd gotten past her rejection years ago. This trip down memory lane was one he'd rather not take.

"Why did you keep it?"

He let his head drop back against the sofa. Why did she always need details about everything? "I stuck it in a drawer at first. Then it was too late to return it."

"I'm sorry." Her words seemed genuine. This had to be as hard for her as it was for him. They needed to move on.

"There's nothing to be sorry about. It's ancient news." He sat up on the edge of the sofa. "We have enough going on right now. I think we can agree to let the past rest."

Thankfully, she followed his lead. "We need to figure out how we're going to handle this new relationship." She spoke every word deliberately and used her hands for emphasis.

"You make it sound like a disease." He chuckled.

"It is a rare condition, if you insist on labeling it." She turned her palms up. "We can call it an engagement, but we need to define how we're going to handle it. With us, and with others. And the kids."

"We agreed that this is a temporary arrangement of commitment between friends."

"Yes, but what are we going to tell our friends? And

the people at church? The kids are young now. They're too young to understand, but we'll have to be careful how we explain our relationship as they get older. We want them to know we're together for them—that we're a family."

"We are a family, Sophie. And we agreed that love is a commitment. They'll grow up watching us committed to them and to each other for their sakes. That's as healthy a relationship as we can hope to have. It's a good thing. And when the judge retires and things *change*, our commitment to be there for each other and the kids won't." He didn't want to say that she could give the ring back then, though he suspected she was thinking the same thing.

"You're right." She rubbed under her eyes with her fingertips, then massaged her temples. "Do you think it would be okay if we don't tell anyone else the details of our situation? Could everyone else just think we got engaged? I can't face having to explain it over and over to the people in our lives."

"If that will make you happy, yes. I don't think our friends will ask. They'll be happy for us and the kids."

Her shoulders relaxed. "You really think so?"

He hoped and prayed he was right.

"I do. And we'll do what you said if anyone asks. We'll tell them we're focusing on the kids." He pulled out his phone and opened the calendar. "Can we say that's settled and move on?"

"Sure." Her tone was shy.

He had to talk about something else—anything else—besides this imitation engagement. Over the years he'd adjusted to the fact that he'd never have the life he'd hoped for. Now he was tied to Sophie, but she wasn't his. Ending this discussion was the best way he knew to keep any unacknowledged pain at bay.

She liked to plan. They could plan. He switched into a matter-of-fact mode and dug into the details they needed to handle. "I want to check in at the store. My staff can handle things, but I still need to go in part-time for a few days while we get settled. We need to decide about living arrangements."

They spent the next hour working through the specifics of merging their lives. It seemed the easiest solution was indeed for Sophie to move into Logan and Caitlyn's house like they'd discussed. Plus, it would be the least disruptive for the kids.

Kevin would come in the mornings before work to help get the kids fed and ready for the day. Sophie would take care of them during the day, working while they napped. Kevin would come after his shift at the store and look after Jade and Carter while she worked. He'd go home when the kids went to bed at night. They'd divide the household chores.

Kevin looked at the notes he'd made on his phone. "I'll get started on the arrangements for moving you in. Some of my staff can help us. We've got boxes at the store, too. We do a big online business now, so I'll have anything you might need."

"I think the budget and figuring out Logan and Caitlyn's finances are top priority for me. That and moving." Sophie seemed like her normal self when she had a project to work on. Maybe by the time they got the move sorted out they'd begin to adjust to sharing their lives. The awkwardness that had settled over him might have lessened by then, too.

Jade's giggle coming from the monitor cut off their discussion.

Sophie smiled. "She's always so happy when she wakes up." She got up from the desk as naturally as if tending to Jade wasn't something she'd just had thrust upon her.

She might think she was afraid of risks, but Sophie Owens was the bravest woman he knew.

A lump formed in his throat. The accident, court, the kids—being engaged to the only woman he'd ever loved and would never marry. It was all too much.

He had to get out of the house. Immediately. "Do you mind if I go to work for a couple of hours? Carter should sleep for most of that time."

"Go ahead. If you want to work through close tonight, I can handle them for the rest of the day." She dismissed his worry about the time with a wave of her hand.

"That would help a lot." He followed her into the large, open-concept living area and grabbed his keys off the kitchen island. "Call if you need me."

Jade called out for Soapy. His need to escape waned as he watched her relaxed approach to being summoned by a three-year-old.

"We'll be fine." She crossed the room to the hall that led to the bedrooms.

"Sophie."

She stopped and turned to face him. "What?"

"Keep the ring. I know you don't want it." He cleared his throat. "But it will show the world how serious we are."

Sophie held her hand in front of her and wiggled her fingers. "Are you sure?"

Kevin could only nod. He was spent, drained beyond any emptiness he'd ever felt. A hollowness filled his chest. He'd made a commitment with no future, and if he weren't so numb, it would hurt as much as their breakup ten years ago.

She clamped her lips together and returned his nod. "You're probably right." Her voice lowered to a whisper. "Thank you."

Jade called Sophie's name again, and she left him standing at the front door.

He wanted her to keep the ring. It would be a constant reminder of his commitment to an engagement for the sake of the children. He decided to think of the engagement as friendly. Something about calling it fake seemed harsh. He and Sophie would deal with its temporary status when the time came.

He'd give his life for those children. So would Sophie. But he wouldn't risk his heart again.

Kevin put on his suit jacket and pulled the engraved wedding band from the inside pocket. He'd thought he might need it in court this morning to secure their guardianship of the children. He held it so the light reflected off the inscription.

My favorite adventure.

The message would always be true, whether Sophie ever saw the ring or not.

Funny, it didn't hurt as much to realize that now as it had for years. He'd accepted their friendship and refused to think of what might have been.

He heard Sophie coming back down the hall toward the living room and slid the ring into his pocket before he stepped outside and locked the door behind him.

The simple act of locking the house reinforced the knowledge that he'd do anything to protect them. Just like he'd locked his heart away, where it would be safe. From danger and pain.

Chapter Four

Carter's cooing turned to crying before Sophie could get to his room the next morning. She'd stepped into the guest room, where her mom was staying, to change into jeans and a casual shirt, thinking Kevin was still in the child's room.

The cries intensified. "I'm coming," she called as she rushed down the hall, wondering where Kevin was.

As Sophie got to the doorway Kevin took Carter from his crib. "Hey, buddy. What's all the fuss about? Uncle K was hurrying. He has to shave every day. Just wait. You'll grow up and have to do the same thing." Kevin teased the tot and carried him to the changing table.

Sophie came into the room. "Hi, Carter." She brushed his rumpled blond hair smooth with her fingers while Kevin wrestled to change the boy's diaper.

A set of fresh clothes laid out for the day surprised her. "I'm impressed, Kevin. You must have done this before you went to bed last night."

Kevin fastened the diaper and tugged off Carter's pajama shirt. "Nope. I did it this morning, but that's a better idea." He tucked squirming arms into sleeves, then pulled the shirt over Carter's round tummy and tickled him. "Look out, little guy. That dinosaur on your shirt might try to eat your breakfast."

"I'll get your sister and meet you both in the kitchen." Carter's cries had turned to giggles, so Sophie headed to Jade's room.

Passing juice cups and cereal bowls to the kids seemed as natural as if she'd done it every day of their lives. Kevin poured her a cup of coffee and set it well out of reach of the little ones before he peeled a banana for Jade.

"Thank you." Sophie poured dry cereal onto the tray of the high chair for Carter. "Who knew there was so much to do in such a short time every morning?" She chuckled when the boy threw his hand across the tray and blew her a kiss, sending little round circles of oats onto the floor. "I love you, too, Carter." She picked up the stray cereal and tossed it in the trash.

"I didn't have a clue." Kevin peeled a banana for himself and sliced it into his cereal bowl. "I don't know how their parents did it."

"Together." Sophie dropped back onto the stool that had already become her regular seat at the island. "I'm sure it took both of them doing everything to get any of it done."

"Well, we're in the deep end, so we may as well swim." He touched the tip of Jade's nose with a finger. "Isn't that right?"

"I have to wear floaties when I swim. Mommy says I'm not big enough to swim by myself, but I am." The little girl didn't stop eating while she talked.

"You'll be bigger this summer. Maybe you can learn to swim without floaties." Kevin smiled at her.

"We'll have to see, Jade." Sophie didn't want Kevin to get her hopes up.

He leaned in and winked at Jade. "I'm a good teacher. We'll make it happen."

Sophie cleared her throat to catch his attention. She gave the slightest shake of her head and hoped he'd get the hint.

He didn't. "What?"

She turned away from Jade and whispered, "We have to be careful not to make promises about things."

Kevin leaned close to her. "Swimming is part of life in Texas. She'll have to learn to swim. It's too dangerous for her not to. There are over a dozen pools in this neighborhood." At least he kept his voice low so Jade couldn't hear.

"I hadn't considered that." Sophie exhaled. "There's so much to think about, but we need to be in agreement before we talk about things in front of the kids. My parents used to call it a 'united front.' It may sound like a battle term, but I'm thinking it's a good idea for co-parenting."

He reached across the island and covered her hand with his. "It's January. We don't have to worry about swimming today."

Diane came into the room in a hurry. Sophie knew her mother saw Kevin withdraw his hand when she approached the island. "Look at all of you. I didn't know breakfast was going to be a family party this morning." She dropped a kiss on the top of Carter's head and cupped Jade's cheek before she popped a bagel into the toaster.

"So, what are the two of you tackling today while I

keep these little ones occupied?" Her mom grabbed a plate from the open dishwasher for her bagel.

Sophie held tight to her coffee mug and tried to relax. "You're a blessing, Mom." She looked at Kevin. "Are you going to the store? I've got to arrange getting out of my lease and all the business side of moving. I have a full list."

He took the last bite of his cereal and nodded. "I told them I'd be in for a few hours every day that I can. They're prepared to cover for me over the next two weeks. I brought a load of boxes from the store and put them in the garage last night. I can run them by your place if you'd like."

"Let me make a few calls first, but that would be a big help."

And just that quickly the changes in her life were set into motion. By nine thirty that morning her lease was canceled and her utilities were scheduled to be disconnected the following week.

She and Kevin left the kids with her mom and drove to her loft. They parked on the street, and he started to unload the boxes from his truck. "I had one of my guys bundle these for me. And I brought tape and packing paper for you."

She reached for a bundle of small boxes at the same time he did, and their shoulders bumped. "Oops." She stumbled backward.

"Careful." He grabbed her arm and steadied her.

"Thanks."

"Are you okay?" His tone revealed a nervousness as deep as her own.

"Sure." She grabbed the boxes. "I don't know why

we're nervous today. We both agreed we're doing the right thing."

He slid a stack of larger boxes to the rear of the truck bed. "Maybe because this is our new reality. I don't know how to act. We had no idea a few days ago that we'd ever be doing this."

"True—and strange." She sighed. They needed to get beyond it. "Do you think we can relax? We've spent a lot of time around each other with Logan and Caitlyn and the kids. Surely we can settle back into that mode."

"Maybe something similar, but I don't think we're ever going back to what we were. About anything." He lifted the bundle and nodded toward the door. "Can you get the door?"

He was right, of course. Everything familiar, except for Logan and Caitlyn, was still there—but it was out of place. *Awkward* wasn't a big enough word.

"Well, since we need to convince everyone that we're engaged, we better figure it out soon."

"I'm on it, boss," he teased as he walked behind her on the sidewalk.

She unlocked the entry to her building and led him up the stairs to her second-floor loft. She put her boxes against the wall outside her door, and he dropped his beside them.

"I'll run down and get the rest of the boxes."

Kevin took the stairs quickly, skipping over several treads on his way down, and she let herself into the loft. He returned from a third trip to the truck just as she slid the last bundle of boxes out of the hallway.

"Thanks for getting the moving supplies for me."

He followed her inside with his load. "I didn't know

how much stuff you had, so if you need more just let me know."

"I will." She placed the large tape dispenser on the kitchen island. "I think I can take it from here. This is one time that I'm glad my tastes lean toward minimalism."

Kevin looked around the loft, and she tried to see her home through his eyes. Lots of open space and brick walls, original to the old building, set the backdrop for her sparse furnishings. Floor-to-ceiling windows on the one exterior wall allowed the morning sun to bathe the room in light. She'd chosen neutral tones for her main pieces and added color to the space with a couple of pillows and some artwork. His gaze halted at her bookcase. "Minimalism? Really?" His lips twisted into a smirk.

"Books don't count."

They both laughed, and she offered him a bottle of water from the refrigerator.

"Well, the books count when you're taking them down the stairs, so I'll have to bring my strongest workers." He took a long drink of water.

"There's a service elevator at the end of the hall."

"What? And you made me drag all those boxes up here?"

She smiled and shrugged.

"I see. Well, your turn will come." He laughed at her, then stopped. "I guess we can fall into a natural friendship if we just relax."

Her heart tripped back into a somber mode. "I guess so." She pulled scissors from the junk drawer in the island and cut the cord that tied the bundle of small boxes together. "I best get busy. Thanks again."

"Let me help you pack. We'll only have your mom's

help with the kids for a few more days. If we work together we can get more done." His idea made sense, but
she'd been looking forward to a few hours alone to think.

"You've got to work. I'll be fine."

He leaned against the island, so close that she had to
stop trying to put the flattened box back together. "I have
staff. They know what's going on." He lifted one corner
of his mouth. "They actually thought I should take a few
days off to celebrate my engagement."

"You told them already?" She hadn't told anyone
other than her mother. Without Caitlyn to confide in,
her circle of confidants was now just her and her mother.
The pain of not sharing what should have been happy
news with her best friend stung again.

Sophie wasn't even sure Caitlyn would think her news
was happy since it was only temporary. Convincing Caitlyn that she and Kevin hadn't had another choice would
have been difficult, but she knew in her heart it was the
right thing to do.

"Of course. We agreed to treat this like a normal
engagement as far as anyone besides the two of us is
concerned. It's the kind of thing you tell people." He
picked up the scissors and cut the cord on a bundle of
large boxes. "You're wearing the ring, so people are
going to ask you. I have to tell my friends and cowork-
ers. It's like ripping off a bandage. The faster you do it,
the less it hurts. And the sooner everyone knows, the
sooner we can move beyond it and not have to talk about
it all the time."

"Okay." The word came out slower than she meant
it to.

"What?" He grabbed the tape dispenser and secured
the bottom of the box he'd folded into shape.

"It just sounds weird when you say it out loud like that."

"It is weird, Soph. And in my experience, the quicker I accept the unexpected, the better." He put a hand on her shoulder. "I promise it won't feel strange forever. It's just you and me and the kids. We've got this."

"Okay." This time she sounded sincere to her own ears. "Then you finish getting these boxes taped, while I pull things out of the cabinets."

In less than an hour they had the kitchen packed. Everything was sorted and stacked near the front door. They worked well together. It was one of the reasons they'd been able to get along with Logan and Caitlyn as friends. When they'd met as a group, each person contributed something different. Logan and Kevin had cooked or grilled, while Caitlyn and Sophie had done dishes and tended to the kids.

When it was just the two of them, Sophie was the organizer and planner, and Kevin was the rapid-fire strength.

"Books next?" Kevin was taping boxes to start on the next room.

Sophie stretched her back. "Coffee first."

"I packed the coffee maker." Kevin frowned.

"And I unpacked it before you sealed the box. It's all about priorities." She snagged the two mugs she'd kept him from packing and made a dark brew.

They sat on opposite ends of her sofa.

"Did you read all of these?" He pointed at the books.

"Yes, I did. All except for that section." She indicated the last two shelves on one side of the bookcase.

He eyed it carefully. "Where are you going to put the bookcase in Logan and Caitlyn's house? It's huge."

Tears pricked her eyes. "I don't know. I was thinking of taking the guest room for myself once Mom leaves. It won't fit there. Maybe I can move things around in the office. Whatever I decide won't include sleeping on the office sofa for one night longer than I have to."

"You don't want the master bedroom?" His tone was soft, showing her that he understood how difficult it must be for her to move into their friends' home.

"I don't. I want them to be there and me to stay here." She exhaled and let her head drop back against the cushions. "I know that's not realistic."

"Jade goes into their room in the middle of the night." His quiet words broke her.

Sophie jerked her head straight. "What?"

"Usually about five o'clock. I think it may be something she's always done."

"And I've never heard her?" Sophie felt her chest tighten and couldn't take a deep breath. "What kind of guardian am I if I can't hear a child roaming from room to room in the middle of the night?" She couldn't keep the tears from falling. "That poor child." Sobs took over where her words ended.

"Hey, hey. You're going to make a great mom, and she's going to be okay." Kevin was suddenly close beside her with an arm around her shoulders. "I heard her every time. Most of the nights, she'd whimper, but she was so sleepy that I was able to carry her back to her room and tuck her in. The longest stretch of her being awake was only a couple of minutes." He rubbed a comforting hand across the back of her shoulders. "That one is a deep sleeper."

"I can't just burst into tears like this. I hate it, and I sure don't want to burden you or the kids with my grief."

Sophie sniffed and dashed a hand across her eyes. "I'm sorry."

"Don't be. It's tough. For all of us. We're going to need each other." He dropped his hand onto his thigh as if he sensed her need to be strong on her own, then leaned in and nudged her shoulder. "Even if it's only for a moment during an outburst."

And there it was again. His ability to distract her from her troubles with a silly move or word. Or both.

"Outburst? You haven't seen a real outburst." She laughed and left him on the sofa. She set her mug in the sink and turned to lean against the counter. "Seriously, Kevin. How did I not hear Jade?"

"First off, she wasn't roaming all over the house. She went to the room next to hers, and you were at the other end of the house in the office. I think the only reason I heard her was because I was so close. The master bedroom door squeaks when you open it. Second, we've all been so overwhelmed that we haven't slept much. I'm sure your body crashed and sent you into a deep sleep."

"*You* woke up." She was the one moving in with the kids, but he was the one who heard them in the night.

"I'm a very light sleeper."

"See. I'm not." Worry knotted her stomach. "There's so much I don't know."

"We're going to learn. Just like Logan and Caitlyn learned." He got up and took his cup to the sink, too. "We know the basics from having spent so much time with the family. We can feed and bathe them and keep them entertained. The rest will come from doing and a lot of prayer."

"You're right." He was getting too close again, leaning against the counter beside her. She needed to stay busy when Kevin was around. Especially when he was being thoughtful, kind Kevin.

She took a step away from him and turned off the coffee maker.

"So, will you take the master?" When she hesitated, he added, "You can put your furniture there. Make it your own."

"Won't that upset the kids? To see us moving their parents' things around?"

"They're so young that they'll adapt quickly to that kind of change, but I think it's a good idea to have them out of the room or asleep when we actually change things that are directly related to Logan and Caitlyn."

"You're probably right. We'll have to make the home ours so we can be comfortable raising the kids there." She took a deep breath. "It's never going to end, is it? The constant bombardment of decisions and changes."

"It will get easier. I don't know when, but I know it will." He walked over to the bookshelf. "So, let's talk about how many of these you want to donate."

"None!"

He laughed and winked at her. "Just as I suspected." He pulled out his phone and sent a text. "I'm having someone bring more boxes. The kind that we get free weights delivered in, so they won't fall apart when we pack all these books in them." He grinned and waved his arm in front of the over-stuffed shelves.

Sophie appreciated his effort to put them both at ease. She had a feeling they'd be tested beyond anything they'd ever imagined by the time Jade and Carter were grown.

Trying when you didn't have to was a sign of great character in her opinion.

Kevin's actions obscured her view of the past.

The thought settled and unsettled her at the same time.

Kevin bounced in place and patted Carter on the back trying to soothe the seemingly endless cries.

"I don't know what's the matter, buddy. You're dry, and you won't eat." He spoke in quiet tones and shushed the boy again. "Please, little man. I don't know what else to do." Kevin prayed silently and paced the living room floor.

Jade tugged on the leg of his jeans. "Uncle K, I can't hear my show. Carter is too loud."

If only it was that easy. He patted Jade on top of the head. "I'm doing my best, but nothing's working. Do you know what Soapy does when he cries like this?" Great. He was asking a three-year-old how to parent.

Jade's little shoulders lifted as if the answer was obvious. "She sings." Her curls swung wide when she pivoted and returned to her spot on the rug in front of the TV, completely uninterested in Kevin's predicament.

"I'm no singer, Carter, but here goes." He was on his second round of a silly song he'd heard Logan sing to the kids when the kitchen door opened and Sophie came in.

"Oh, no. Are you a sad boy?" she cooed at Carter and dropped the grocery bags she carried onto the island.

Kevin walked toward her with more relief than he wanted to acknowledge. "Nothing I do is working. Do you think he might be sick?" Carter lunged for Sophie as soon as she was within reach.

"Poor baby. Is Uncle K's singing making you cry?" She nestled Carter into her embrace and went to the refrigerator.

"Hey. Singing was Jade's idea." He dropped onto a stool at the island. "He's been crying like that for ten minutes." His futile efforts to ease the child had left him feeling helpless.

Sophie pulled a plastic dinosaur out of the refrigerator and handed it to Carter. "Here you go. Are those teeth bothering you?"

Carter grabbed the toy and chewed on it like a lifeline. His sobs slowed to grousing.

"Kevin, will you get his musical lamb out of the crib?" Why hadn't he thought of that?

"Sure." He came back into the living room and offered it to her.

She refused and pointed to Logan's chair. "You sit there. I'll give him to you."

"No." He gave a slow, dramatic shake of his head. "I am *not* who he wants." If Carter wanted Sophie, Kevin could admit it.

For a minute he thought she was going to laugh at him. "That's why it has to be you." She raised her brows and waited.

Then it dawned on him that she was making a point to Kevin and Carter. "Aha." He sat in the chair and reached for the child. "Let's try this again." Carter grunted his disapproval, then changed his mind when Kevin pressed the lamb's tummy to activate the music. He settled in and chewed on the chilled teether.

Funny how a child who was inconsolable before could quickly relax into his arms. There was something right about being there for these kids, even when it was so hard. He was grateful that Sophie made him see the importance of being the one to get Carter settled.

"Here." Sophie tossed Kevin a burp cloth. "He started

drooling during the day. I'm sorry I didn't warn you that he's cutting his molars."

Kevin wiped Carter's face and hands, careful not to dislodge the dinosaur. "How did you know that was the problem?"

"Google." She was unpacking the groceries and putting everything away.

Watching her do the menial task caught his attention. The way she moved around the kitchen as if she'd lived in the house for ages stirred a sense of home in him that he'd never experienced. A sense he must deny. They'd only started packing the things in her loft the day before, and it wasn't for the sake of making a home with him. It never would be.

That day together had been easier than he'd expected. Working on a common goal kept them focused. They could do this. He was beginning to see that raising the kids wouldn't be as impossible as he'd feared in the beginning. Apparently, she was taking it in stride if she only needed an internet search to fix things.

All he had to do was remember that she was his temporary fiancée and not his future wife.

"Google? Really?"

"Whatever works." She folded the reusable grocery bags and put them away. "I bought a rotisserie chicken for dinner. Do you want me to make some pasta to go with it?"

"You want to cook? I thought we agreed that I'd cook." Her lack of kitchen prowess had been a running joke for years. Anytime they'd come to this house for a meal, Sophie had been asked to bring drinks or chips. Caitlyn would occasionally ask her to bring a roll of cookie dough, always insisting that Sophie not actually bake the cookies.

He hoped teasing her would help to reinforce the normality of their friendship in his mind.

"I can boil water as good as anyone." She pretended to be offended. "Besides, I thought you might be tired from your afternoon at the store. I didn't know Mom was going to leave the kids with you as soon as you got here."

"She didn't want to, but I told her I've got to learn to handle them on my own. I may as well start now." Carter had calmed down, so Kevin put him on the rug next to Jade and joined Sophie in the kitchen.

She stopped and looked at the kids. "They had a good day, I think. Mom said they napped and played while I was at my place packing more of my stuff."

Kevin pulled a pot from the cabinet and filled it with water. "That's good. Your mom will be back for dinner. She's running some errands for herself. I asked if she can watch the kids Saturday afternoon while we move your things. I've got a crew lined up."

"That's so quick. I don't know if we'll be ready."

He agreed with her. Most days his head was spinning with the details of what they had to do. "We don't have a choice. Your mom goes back to work Monday and won't be available to help as much after that." He salted the water and put it on the stove to boil.

"Wait a minute." Sophie turned a puzzled face to him. "You're *planning* this? I thought you were Mr. Spontaneous. Where is all this organization coming from?"

He couldn't stop himself from grinning at her. Part of him enjoyed the surprise on her face. He liked the idea that he wasn't like one of her books—read and put on the shelf to keep for the memories, but lacking any future secrets. "You don't know everything about me."

She rolled her eyes. "I know you're not organized."

"You know I'm spontaneous. I am, however, also a business owner. And planning is a strategic part of my everyday life now."

She laughed. "That had to hurt."

"What?"

"Finding out that you had to be organized."

He shrugged. "Well, I usually let my assistant manager do the bulk of it."

A knock at the door kept her from teasing him more. Her mother came in and took over with the kids while he cooked. Sophie disappeared into the office to work.

Next week it would be just him and Sophie with the kids. The extra work of rearranging their lives had to be done quickly, because he could already see that raising two kids would consume their time and energy.

He wasn't ready.

Lord, help us to get it right.

The silent prayer was one of the many he'd offered in the last few days. It was the only way he'd survive this new life.

Chapter Five

Sophie taped another box closed and pushed it toward the bedroom door. Every box of Logan and Caitlyn's clothes and personal items reminded her of the days she'd helped her mother pack away her father's things. The pain was fresh and raw.

And complicated by the sound of Kevin's voice as he occupied the children in the living room. She'd worked on her business accounts while he'd cooked, and now she needed to get the master bedroom ready for the move in two days.

It was hard work. Physically. And emotionally.

Kevin was laughing and playing while she mourned.

That wasn't a fair thought, but she couldn't help it. Death always reminded her of how much she missed her dad, especially his smile and how he'd always been quick with a hug whenever she'd needed it. Part of her would miss him forever. Ten years couldn't fade the memory of that love.

It had eased the pain, though. Most of her memories were happy. The pain hadn't flooded back in a long time, until Logan and Caitlyn died.

Jade squealed in delight. Carter's lower chuckle joined in. They sure were having a good time. Kevin had been right to keep them entertained while she changed things in the master bedroom. He'd joined them on the living room floor after dinner while her mother did the dishes. Sophie had been busy for the last hour.

Lord, help me to honor the memory of their parents in ways that lets the children know how much their parents loved them.

She put another box together and stepped back into the closet. She'd pulled several of the clothes they'd worn the most and set them aside. Trying not to think too much, she tucked the clothes into the box. Her mother had told her about a friend who made memory quilts. Sophie decided to have one made for each child.

"Soapy!" Jade and Kevin called her name.

In an instant, the moment for mourning was replaced by responsibility and, hopefully, a few moments of joy while she helped Kevin put the kids to bed.

They were doing this. Every day the chores for the kids became more routine.

The joy the children brought into her life would help her heal from the loss of her friends. She knew that. Even as she hated the reality, she knew God had given her and Kevin those kids for a reason.

God had also given Carter and Jade the only guardians who would love them like she and Kevin would.

She pushed aside the box of clothes for the memory quilts and left the room, closing the door on the pain and turning to embrace the future.

Saturday came and went too quickly, but Sophie had managed to get everything packed and ready for the move. She'd even finished sorting everything in what was now her room, so the men Kevin arranged to help them had been able to put things in the right rooms when they'd unloaded the truck.

Chad Weston, Kevin's assistant manager, was the last to leave. "See you Monday, boss." He closed the door as he left Logan and Caitlyn's house.

Sophie called out her thanks just in time for him to hear it, then collapsed onto the sectional in the living room. "I can't do another thing. How can a moving day have more than twenty-four hours in it?"

"It's not my fault you have more books than the library." Kevin handed her a cold canned drink and dropped into Logan's chair. "We'd have finished an hour ago if that bookcase hadn't weighed a ton." She'd have known he was teasing her without his quick wink and sly grin.

"Well, maybe all you sporting types should up your weight lifting game."

"Yes, ma'am. As soon as I heal." He groaned and rubbed both upper arms in exaggerated pain.

"We'd never have finished without all the help you arranged. Chad and the guys were awesome." She opened the can and enjoyed the burn of the bubbles as she quenched her thirst.

"My store crew is a great group. They're always up for a challenge. Even the ones who kept the store open while we moved your things knew they were helping me."

"Please thank them for me." She drew in a deep breath and prepared herself for more work. Moving never ended in a day. "I'm not sure how long we have until Mom returns with the kids. I want to get my room in some sort of order before they see it."

"They're going to eat dinner with the pastor and his family before they come home at about seven thirty."

Sophie shook her head. "You really did think of everything." His kindness was a basic part of his character. Even as a kid, he'd been the one to make sure others were included and having fun. She still admired this authentic part of him that had endured into adulthood. She pushed herself off the sofa. "That gives me a couple of hours, so I better get started."

"I'll help move the boxes around for you, but you're on your own when you start unpacking them." He followed her down the hall.

In less than an hour they had order restored to the space. Kevin's employees had stacked most of the boxes in the closet, so it didn't take long to get the room ready for her first night.

She tossed a set of fresh sheets onto the mattress. "I'll order us a pizza and then make the bed. That'll be the end of it for today."

"I've got dinner handled. It's not pizza, but you'll like it." He nodded toward the door. "I'll let you finish here." He whistled as he walked down the hall.

Kevin made the transition easier. How did he know just the right things to do to alleviate some of the stress? Handling where her mom and the kids would spend the afternoon, lining up a moving crew—even boxes and tape. And he topped it off with a meal.

Mr. Spontaneous was proving himself to be indispensable. She hoped he thought she was pulling her weight, too. A good night's rest on her own mattress should help with her energy levels. She arranged the pale gray and blue pillows on the white quilt.

It was a start to making the place feel like her home.

"Come and get it." Kevin called out from the kitchen, and she laughed. His constant motion and noise were both annoying and refreshing sometimes.

"Chopsticks or a fork?" Kevin held up both for Sophie to choose.

"Fork."

"Soy sauce, right?"

"Yes." She filled water glasses for both of them. They sat at the island, and he offered a quick prayer of thanks for their food and the safe completion of the day's work.

"I love Japanese food." Sophie tore open several sauce packets.

"I know it's your go-to comfort food, and since I happen to be as exhausted as you, I ordered takeout."

"How do you remember so much? We haven't had this kind of food together in ages." She twisted on her stool to look at him.

"I know a lot about you." He shrugged. "Like how early you'll get up tomorrow so we can get those little ones ready for church. Probably without letting your mother help."

"You'd be right. If we let her help, we won't know that we can handle it after she's gone." She smiled. "I didn't realize I was so predictable."

"*Reliable* is the word I'd use."

"Hmm. I'll take it." She put her fork down. "We've been so busy getting me settled this week that we haven't talked a lot about what you need."

"I did think of one thing I'd like to do." He'd been

pondering it and wanted to be careful how he approached her. "I know you've agreed to live here, and it's the right thing."

"Okay?" The question in the word was bigger than the word itself.

"Well, there will be times, in the course of the future…" He cleared his throat.

"Just say it." There it was. Her insistence on the bottom line, as if all of life were a math problem to be solved by a known formula.

"I want to set up the guest room for me. I'd like to be able to take overnight shifts with the kids and let you have the night off when you want it." He braced himself for her objections.

"I told you we can't share the house." She wasn't argumentative. Argumentative would have involved some give and take. She wasn't giving or taking. She was entrenched.

"I don't mean to share the house. I can stay here while you visit with your girlfriends."

"Caitlyn was the only girlfriend I did things like that with." Sadness clouded her eyes again. "But thanks for the offer."

"You and your mom like to go to the movies. I heard her telling you about that movie based on some romantic classic that's coming out in the spring. The two of you could go to the movie and dinner."

"I can do that without you sleeping over."

"You can stay at your mom's overnight. Get a full night's rest. Let me be with the kids."

"Why?"

He dropped his chopsticks into his bowl of rice. "Because your life as you know it can't stop because of the kids. We're both going to need to do things that don't involve them. Logan went camping with me. Caitlyn went shopping in Dallas with you. If they took time away, we should admit that we'll need that, too."

He didn't want to feel like a part-time guardian. If he only came in and out of the house, the kids would see Sophie as a parent, but not so much him. She had to give on this.

"I was just thinking if I had a room set up here, it would be easier for all of us. I want the kids to see me as a real father figure. I need to have a permanent place in what's essentially *our* family home. It may even help with the home inspections that the court ordered."

There. He'd said it. "We have to consider more than right now and what the kids need. We both have certain things that we'll need. I still have to go on excursions for work. Some of them take place on weekends, so I won't be here then. You'll need the same kind of freedom."

"I get it." Her shoulders slumped. "It will be a long time before I'm ready to do anything like that."

"Okay, then." He covered her hand on the kitchen island and instantly wished he hadn't. He couldn't snatch his hand away. Comforting her—making today as easy as possible—had somehow become more important to him than he realized. Instead of pulling away, he squeezed her hand ever so lightly. She responded in kind.

The doorbell rang. Three times in rapid succession.

Sophie looked into his eyes. "Looks like our family is home."

The words burrowed their way into his closed heart—a heart her rejection had sealed. He never intended to open it again.

* * *

The next morning he lowered the garage door before he backed out of the driveway to follow Caitlyn's SUV to the church. Sophie and her mother rode ahead of him with the kids.

It had taken two hours to get everyone fed and dressed for morning services. At one point he'd been ready to skip going and instead watch the service online, but Sophie insisted that Jade and Carter needed to be around their friends.

She was right, of course, but it didn't make it any easier.

At the church, everyone was kind. Too kind. Over and over again, people offered their condolences on the loss of Logan and Caitlyn.

The hardest part had been answering the congratulations from everyone who had heard about their engagement. One friend of Sophie's had seen the ring when they'd walked into the lobby. That was all it took. It was like watching fire sweep across a dry field. Nothing could stop its spread. By the time they'd dropped the kids off in their respective classes, Kevin felt as if everyone in the world knew his most personal business.

The pastor clapped him on the shoulder. "Congrats, Kevin. I know the two of you will be very happy together."

He couldn't think of anything to say that wouldn't be an outright lie—or, at the very least, a distortion of the truth. "Thanks." He dug one finger into the collar of his shirt and pulled. It couldn't be shrinking while he wore it, yet the fact that he suddenly needed more air was real.

Sophie came up beside him and slipped her hand into the crook of his other elbow. The comfort of her action clashed with the surprise of it. "Thank you, Pastor." She smiled at Mark Gillis. "If you'll excuse us, we don't want to be late for our class." She tugged on his arm and led him down a quiet hallway.

As soon as they were out of earshot, he stopped. She dropped her hand as he thanked her.

"I'm sorry, Sophie. I knew that was coming, but for some reason I wasn't ready. I usually come to church for solace and comfort, not prepared for a tidal wave of questions and congratulations."

"Well, the quicker it spreads, the quicker we'll be done with all the explaining."

Her long hair hung loose around her shoulders. It was perfect with the cream sweater she'd put on just before they left the house. She was so beautiful. It wasn't a bad thing for her to be on his arm at church. Together. That's what they were.

Only they weren't. They were together with the kids, but the enormity of this temporary, necessary engagement hit him with unexpected force today.

"I hope it spreads far and wide today then, because I don't want to do this again." He frowned at her, drawn back to what she had told their pastor. "We're not in the same class."

"I think we should be. People will expect us to be together. Caitlyn always told me that she and Logan loved the couples' class."

"Couples? Uh, no." He took a step back and held up both hands without even thinking about it.

"Wait." She tilted her head to one side and gave him her think-about-it look. "There are a lot of young couples in there. People who are dealing with the same things we're dealing with now. Caitlyn said it was a great class for parenting and—"

"Aha! I thought so. Parenting and marriage. That's what you were going to say."

"Relationships. You know, like the two of us." She wagged one finger back and forth between the two of them. "In a committed relationship."

Two kids ran down the hall, and she moved closer to him to avoid a collision with the children.

With no argument against her logic, he stuck his elbow out for her hand and took a deep breath when she stepped to his side.

A mistake. The tropical scent of her shampoo filled his senses.

Focus, Kevin. And remember to keep some space between the two of you.

He cleared his throat. "We better hurry then, so we don't walk in late and disrupt the class."

Kevin wished a disrupted class was his biggest hurdle.

Daily disruptions changed every aspect of his life now. Protecting himself from unnecessary pain kicked in like a reflex.

It was one thing to answer a lot of engagement questions without giving up too much information. He could do that.

Keeping his raw and wounded heart safe from Sophie while allowing those little kids in to help them heal was another matter entirely.

Chapter Six

Sophie couldn't relax during the Sunday morning class. No matter how she shifted in her chair, her shoulder bumped against Kevin's. Everywhere she looked someone was looking back.

Jackson Yarbrough taught the couples class. He'd opened with a prayer for Jade and Carter, as well as Sophie and Kevin. Many of the attendees shared sympathy over the loss of Logan and Caitlyn. It was getting to her.

She reached for her bag on the floor and dug out a tissue. When she sat up again, Kevin had rested his arm along the back of her chair. He gave her shoulders a gentle hug. It was a gesture meant to comfort, and it was almost more than she could take.

Her involuntary shift away from his embrace caused him to withdraw and edge away from her. He couldn't move far because the class was full of young couples. The rows and chairs were situated as close together as possible to accommodate the group.

She forced herself to listen to Jackson speak and realized he'd earned his reputation as a popular teacher. He related well to the people who came every Sunday for a Bible lesson directed at their daily struggles. Under different circumstances, she'd admire the way he let his natural humor help keep the class engaged. Today, too many thoughts and emotions pressed against her heart and shattered her focus.

Just when Sophie thought she might have to walk out of the classroom to get some fresh air, Jackson said, "And if you don't believe me, just ask my wife. She'll back me up. Right, Allison?"

"Sure, sweetie. Whatever you say." Jackson's wife's response had the class laughing out loud at a joke Sophie completely missed.

The disruption in the quiet gave her a chance to get a grip on her emotions. She turned to see if Kevin was laughing and caught him watching her.

He leaned close to her. "Do you want to leave? We can." His whisper was intimate and caring.

It soothed her raw nerves. *No.* She mouthed the word.

"Are you okay?" he whispered.

"I am now." She nodded. "But I have no idea what was so funny."

He lifted his brows and shrugged. "Me, either."

That short exchange of words needed no explanation and broke the tension that her rejection of his touch had caused.

Kevin relaxed in his chair, and the class continued as if nothing in the world had changed. As if two of their classmates hadn't died. As if tomorrow would come and life would go on.

Sophie knew it would. And she knew coming into this new class was the right thing for her and Kevin. Even though their engagement would be short-lived, they had a lifetime of parenting ahead of them. It was another step toward the future that was fast becoming the present.

Even when the class was laughing while she wept inside, she was grateful for her church. They all came together from different situations in life and shared the love of a family.

That love would get them through the changes they faced.

No matter what.

Monday morning was chaotic.

"Mom, are you leaving now?" Sophie buckled Carter in his high chair, more to keep him from wandering off again than anything else.

"I'll be late if I don't leave now." Diane blew a kiss to Carter and waved at Sophie. She opened the door to leave, and Kevin was there with his hands too full to knock. "Say a prayer. You're gonna need it."

Kevin's eyes grew wide as he turned to Sophie. "What did she mean?" He closed the door behind him with his foot.

Jade yelled from her room. "Soapy! I can't find it." Wails of unhappiness followed.

"I'm coming, sweetie." Sophie patted Carter on the head.

"Can you pour some cereal on his tray while I help her find that doll she sleeps with? It's missing and she's having a fit." She took off down the hall, knowing he would jump right in to help.

Five minutes later, she carried Jade to the kitchen island and put her on her stool. The little girl's face was red from crying, but there was a smile there, too. "You put Rosie right beside you, and I'll get your breakfast."

"All done." Kevin put a pink plate in front of Jade. "I thought you might like your favorite cinnamon roll today." He winked at Jade, who smiled back at him.

"Bluebewwy muffin is my new favorite." Jade touched the roll and licked the icing from her fingertip. "But I still like cinnamon rolls a lot."

"You saved the day, Uncle K." Sophie hadn't had a minute's peace since she'd woken up.

"And for you, Soapy." He held out a large coffee cup from Cup o' Caff.

"Thank you! Look, kids, Uncle K knows Soapy's favorite, too." She read the ticket on the side of the cup in surprise. "With extra cream. You are good."

"Cream, no sugar. As always." He pointed at the bag on the counter. "There's a bagel in there for you. Carter ate a biscuit."

She opened the bag. "What about you?"

Kevin lifted his coffee cup. "My bagel smelled so good that I ate it in the truck on my way here."

"You have no idea how much I appreciate this. It's been quite a morning already, and I haven't unpacked my coffee machine yet." She didn't realize how quickly things could unravel if any one piece of the kids' routine was out of place. Jade's missing doll had upset the delicate balance of getting everyone dressed and fed.

"There's a coffee maker on the counter." He looked at his watch. "And it's eight thirty."

"I know what time it is. I'm usually well into my workday by now." She rolled her eyes. "But *my* coffee machine is how I manage that. Let's just say it's fancy."

"A fancy coffee maker for a woman who drinks coffee with cream." He wiped Carter's hands and mouth. "An accountant at that."

"Hey. That coffee machine works wonders. It was a splurge. I'm single, so I can do that. Just like you and your fancy sunglasses."

They stopped and stared at each other. They weren't those carefree people anymore.

She broke eye contact first. No need to dwell on what was, when what is was waiting to be changed into fresh clothes. She took Jade to her room while Kevin took care of Carter.

Sophie had been up early and dressed before the kids made a sound. It was the only way she knew to stay ahead of them. The fact that she didn't want Kevin showing up at the door and finding her in a T-shirt and yoga pants with her hair all over the place had helped to motivate her.

The four of them were back in the living room a few minutes later. Jade was playing with Rosie on the sectional, and Carter chewed on plastic blocks on the rug in front of the fireplace.

"Are you okay to handle them alone today? You look tired."

"Thanks." She grimaced as soon as the word left her lips. "I'm sorry. I know you're just being nice."

"I'm trying to be helpful, not just nice." He grinned. "It's new. Work with me."

She slumped onto a stool and picked up her coffee. "Let's just say Jade was true to form and woke me sometime around three. It took an hour to get her settled, and it was another hour before I went back to sleep."

"Ouch." He pointed at her cup. "Maybe next time, I'll have them add an extra shot of espresso."

"Could you?" They laughed, and she checked her watch. "There's one thing for certain. I'm blowing away my fitness goals. I didn't know I could get in so many steps so early."

"An upside." He looked over at the children. "You can call if you need me. Anytime."

"Thanks, but we've got to get used to our new reality. You go to work. We'll be fine here." She walked him to the door. "If you have a sofa in your office, you might want to grab a nap instead of lunch. They're all yours when you get back."

"Bye, kids." He waved at the two of them.

Sophie's heart squeezed a bit when Carter said, "Bye, K." Jade made Rosie blow him a kiss.

"I'll call and check on you guys during the day."

Though he was sweet to offer, Sophie felt she had to do this herself. They'd planned everything. It was time to work the plan.

"You don't have to do that. We're good."

"Okay." Sophie heard the faint disappointment in his voice. He was in his truck before she realized that she'd rejected his offer of help.

He'd taken it personally.

She'd have to be more careful. They were all hurting. Her, Kevin and the kids.

She'd only meant to keep him from feeling responsible for them while he was at work—not to add to his pain.

In reality, he was responsible—24/7. She knew she'd never go anywhere again and leave the kids behind without wondering what they were doing and if they were safe and happy.

Kevin's offer to call proved the depth of his commitment.

She pulled out her phone and typed a text.

Call whenever you want. I'll be glad to let you know how the kids are. Video call if you want.

She was proofing the message when Jade cried out in pain. Carter had thrown one of his toys and hit his sister in the arm. Sophie hurried to make sure Jade wasn't hurt, then went about her first morning with full care of both kids. The day passed in a rush of chores, lunch and snacks. The only time Sophie had to herself was during the afternoon when both children napped.

She wondered why Kevin hadn't called. It was almost time for him to arrive before she realized she'd never sent the message.

He hadn't called, and it was her fault.

That afternoon Kevin pushed open the front door of the house with his foot and wondered why it wasn't fully closed. "Hi, honey. I'm home."

The minute he saw Sophie's face, he knew she didn't like his joke.

"Uh-oh." He set the grocery bags he carried on the counter and held out his hands to take Carter from her. "Hey, big guy. Come here."

Carter lunged into his arms and giggled.

"What's going on?" Kevin gave the child's cheeks a playful squeeze. "Have you guys been giving Soapy a hard time today?"

"Soapy." Carter pointed at her.

Strands of Sophie's ponytail hung loose in her face, and she blew at them. "Ugh." She snatched the elastic band out of her hair and gathered it all together, twisting it into place again. Her hair wasn't much neater, but, even flustered, she was pretty. "I'm sorry. You caught me trying to get them to eat their dinner. It seems I don't know how to do anything right."

Jade walked over and tugged on the side of his jeans. "She cut up my b'sgetti. I'm not a baby. Mommy says I'm a big girl."

"And big girls eat long spaghetti?" Kevin smiled down at her, then looked at Sophie. "I'm guessing the little guy joined in on the fuss."

"Apparently he doesn't want noodles tonight."

"Sorry for the hassle, but I'm supposed to cook. You didn't have to worry about it." First, she didn't want him to call, and now she was taking over the tasks they'd agreed were his.

Sophie looked at the kitchen clock. "It was getting late, and they were hungry. Caitlyn always said pasta was something they both love to eat."

"You knew I was going for groceries after work. I didn't realize how long it would take. There are a lot of things on the list that I've never bought before. Like diapers." He was doing his best and didn't want her to be frustrated.

"I'm not upset with you. Just tired, I guess."

"Well, you go do what you need to, and I'll take it from here." He put Carter in his high chair. "Why was the front door open?"

"Open?" Sophie's bewildered expression deepened. "I don't know." She looked at Jade. "Did you open the door?"

Jade was suddenly quiet and scooted behind Kevin.

Sophie squatted beside her and reached out her hand. "It's okay to tell me." Kindness filled her tone.

Jade snuggled closer to Kevin, and he leaned over to put his hand on her back. "What is it?"

"I heard Daddy's car. Mommy lets me open the door for him." Her bottom lip trembled. "It was you." She pointed at Kevin.

In an instant he and Sophie wrapped Jade in a hug. "You sweet girl, I'm so sorry." Kevin kissed the top of Jade's head.

"I want Daddy to come home." Sobs racked the child's body. Just that quickly the three of them were in tears.

"I know, baby." Sophie pulled Jade against her and dropped down to sit on the floor. "I know." She caressed the child's back in an effort to soothe her.

Carter reacted to his sister's breakdown with a scream followed by tears and flailing arms. Kevin scooped him up and paced the living room in an effort to calm him.

He met Sophie's gaze over the top of Jade's head. They were locked together in heartbreak.

Suddenly he remembered Logan trying to get Carter out of a bad mood one day a few weeks earlier. At this point, he'd try anything. He slid his hands under the child's arms and hoisted him into the air. "Do you wanna fly?"

Carter swallowed a gasp. "F'y!"

Kevin swooped him high and then low as he moved around the living area. Carter began to giggle. Jade stopped crying and looked up. Sophie wiped tears away from her face and Jade's.

"Me, too!" Jade scrambled to her feet and started jumping up and down as she reached for Kevin.

"Soapy?" He gave her a silent plea for help, and she nodded.

"I've got you, girl." She lifted Jade into her arms. "You're a rocket. Swoosh!"

The next two minutes were filled with laughs and giggles. Crisis calmed. For the moment.

Sophie landed with Jade on the sectional, and Kevin brought Carter in with a final dip to sit next to them.

"Let's feed these fliers." He offered Sophie his hand. She laughed and let him tug her off the sofa.

"Let's." She went back to the stove and scooped up fresh noodles for Jade.

Kevin toasted slices of bread to go with the pasta. "I'm sorry you had such a rough day."

"It wasn't as bad as it seemed when you came in. Just more than I expected. There wasn't time to make a phone call or answer an email." Sophie's cheeks went pink. "I'm sorry I lost it."

He buttered the toast and added it to the plates she'd prepared. "I think this is why God had Logan and Caitlyn choose both of us. This is a two-person responsibility. We'll get better at it. I promise."

She offered him a gentle smile. "I think the learning curve is steeper than I expected."

"Don't worry." He picked Carter up and put him back in the high chair. "Come eat your dinner, Jade. If you and your brother eat your pasta with a happy face, then we'll all go to Scoopdilyicious for ice cream."

"Yay!" Jade climbed onto her stool and picked up the pink fork that matched her princess plate. "Carter, eat good." She started trying to twirl her spaghetti.

Kevin ruffled her hair. "That's my girl."

"Really?" Sophie leaned against the counter near the sink. She wasn't angry, but he knew she wouldn't have bribed the kids like he did. "Ice cream?"

He shrugged. "It's all I could think of. You know I was never a quick learner. That curve is gonna take me some time, but one day I'll have them eating protein bars and drinking smoothies."

She raised her brows and sighed. "At least they're eating."

Minutes later Kevin wished he'd factored in how close it was to their bedtime and how hungry he was before he'd promised to take them out. Neither he nor Sophie had eaten a bite before the kids finished and were circling his legs. Jade clapped her hands and squealed. "I want 'nilla ice c'eam."

Sophie seemed to read his thoughts. "It's late. Maybe we should go tomorrow."

"But…Soapy—" Jade's chubby cheeks framed her pink frown. "Uncle K said."

Kevin cut his eyes at Sophie and hoped she would agree. "I think we need a treat, Soapy."

"Okay." Her agreement came, fatigue probably having made the choice for her.

"Yay! Ice c'eam!" Jade's excitement was contagious.

As if on cue, Carter clapped his hands, and they all laughed for the second time that day. With the laughter came a bit of relief from the overwhelming tension.

Sophie smiled at Kevin. Her brown eyes were filled with sadness and a need for hope. "A trip to Scoopdilyicious always makes me feel better." She touched his sleeve and whispered, "Thank you."

Kevin helped Sophie load the kids into Caitlyn's SUV and drove them to the ice-cream shop. "I think I need an ice-cream sundae. Maybe one of their specialty ones. The salted caramel might be just the thing."

"That sounds like a healthy dinner," Sophie teased, and got out of the vehicle.

Each of them took a child from the back seat, and

Kevin grabbed the bag she'd filled with anything they might need. Inside, they settled into a booth with Jade in the corner beside Sophie and Carter in a high chair at the end of the table.

Nancy, the owner of Scoopdilyicious, approached them wearing a bright pink apron that bore her name and the ice-cream cone logo of the shop. "Hello to all of you." Her smile was sweet and included the children. Then she looked at Sophie with the same sadness that had filled every expression he and Sophie had seen in the days since the accident. Gran Colina was a small town that lived up to the ideal of being close and caring—a place where privacy was rare and compassion was the norm. "It's a good night for ice cream. What can I get for everyone?"

Jade jumped in first. "I want 'nilla in a big cone." She held her little hands up to show a size bigger than any ice-cream cone had ever been.

Kevin grinned. "Do you want sprinkles and chocolate chips, too?"

Jade shook her head. "Mommy says I can't have both." Her lower lip quivered. "I want Mommy!" She flung herself into Sophie's arms and cried.

"I know you do, baby." Sophie rubbed Jade's back in the same soothing circles she'd used to calm the child earlier.

Nancy slipped away from the table and the intimate moment.

Kevin mouthed, *I'm sorry.*

Sophie gave him a forced smile while Carter played with the purple plastic spoon Nancy had given him on their arrival.

Jade sniffed and pushed away from Sophie. "I'm sad."

FREE BOOKS GIVEAWAY

2 FREE ROMANCE BOOKS!

2 FREE SUSPENSE BOOKS!

GET UP TO FOUR FREE BOOKS & TWO FREE GIFTS WORTH OVER $20!

We pay for everything!

Dear Reader,

I am writing to announce the launch of a huge **FREE BOOK GIVEAWAY**... and to let you know that YOU are entitled to choose up to FOUR fantastic books that WE pay for.

Try **Love Inspired® Romance Larger-Print** books and fall in love with inspirational romances that take you on an uplifting journey of faith, forgiveness and hope.

Try **Love Inspired® Suspense Larger-Print** books where courage and optimism unite in stories of faith and love in the face of danger.

Or TRY BOTH!

In return, we ask just one favor: Would you please participate in our brief Reader Survey? We'd love to hear from you.

This FREE BOOKS GIVEAWAY means that we pay for *everything!* We'll even cover the shipping, and no purchas is necessary, now or later. So please return your survey today. You'll get **Two Free Books** and **Two Mystery Gifts** from each series to try, altogether worth over **$20!**

Sincerely

Pam Powers

Pam Powers
For Harlequin Reader Servic

Complete the survey below and return it today to receive up to 4 FREE BOOKS and FREE GIFTS guaranteed!

FREE BOOKS GIVEAWAY
Reader Survey

1
Do you prefer books which reflect Christian values?

○ YES ○ NO

2
Do you share your favorite books with friends?

○ YES ○ NO

3
Do you often choose to read instead of watching TV?

○ YES ○ NO

YES! Please send me my Free Rewards, consisting of **2 Free Books from each series I select** and **Free Mystery Gifts**. I understand that I am under no obligation to buy anything, as explained on the back of this card.

❑ Love Inspired® Romance Larger-Print (122/322 IDL GQ36)
❑ Love Inspired® Suspense Larger-Print (107/307 IDL GQ36)
❑ Try Both (122/322 & 107/307 IDL GQ4J)

FIRST NAME	LAST NAME

ADDRESS

APT.#	CITY

STATE/PROV.	ZIP/POSTAL CODE

EMAIL ❑ Please check this box if you would like to receive newsletters and promotional emails from Harlequin Enterprises ULC and its affiliates. You can unsubscribe anytime.

LI/LIS-520-FBG21

▲ If offer card is missing write to: Harlequin Reader Service, P.O. Box 1341, Buffalo, NY 14240-8531 or visit www.ReaderService.com ▼

BUSINESS REPLY MAIL
FIRST-CLASS MAIL   PERMIT NO. 717   BUFFALO, NY

POSTAGE WILL BE PAID BY ADDRESSEE

HARLEQUIN READER SERVICE
PO BOX 1341
BUFFALO NY 14240-8571

NO POSTAGE
NECESSARY
IF MAILED
IN THE
UNITED STATES

Kevin reached across the table and grabbed her tiny fist. "We all are."

He thought it was important to acknowledge Jade's pain instead of brushing it off with a platitude about how everything would be all right. Too many people dismissed the feelings of children as inconsequential. Jade and Carter were hurting more than anyone. He wouldn't dismiss that. Ever.

"You know what, Jade." Sophie tweaked Jade's nose. "I think—because you're so sad—this time Mommy would want you to have both. Sprinkles *and* chocolate chips." In contrast to the woman who'd been falling apart an hour ago, Sophie's maternal instincts kicked in as if she'd had years of practice.

"Really?" Jade played with the ends of Sophie's hair.

"Yes."

Kevin admired the way Sophie made the exception— one of many that night. How long would it be until they were all at ease? Weeks? Months? He prayed for the day as much as he dreaded it. When the pain lessened, they'd be accustomed to not having Logan and Caitlyn around. Moving forward seemed traitorous even though he knew it was necessary.

Jade scrambled back onto her side of the bench seat. "So, you and Uncle K can have extra, 'cause you're both sad, too."

"You're right. We are." Kevin nodded his agreement, and Jade grabbed the book Sophie had laid on the table for her. She flipped the heavy pages, instantly involved in the story.

The conversation had been intense, and then it was over. The child had been promised a treat and was content again.

"Her resilience is amazing." Sophie's words mirrored his thoughts.

"It really is." He picked at the corner of his thumb-nail. "Are you doing better?"

She nodded. "For now."

"You're better at this parenting thing than you know." Sophie exhaled a slow breath. "I'm doing my best."

He wanted to hold her hand across the table and reas-sure her, but she wasn't his to hold. She looked lonely. "I'm here for you."

Her closed lips tried to force a smile and failed. Her eyes never left his. Everything faded away except their promise to work together. They each knew how com-mitted the other was.

Only now were they beginning to see the enormity of the task ahead of them.

Nancy came back to the table, and the moment was over. The everyday world interrupted, and they ordered enough ice cream to make everyone forget the troubles of the day—or at least numb the pain for a few minutes.

An hour and a half later the kids were snoozing in their beds. Kevin closed the dishwasher and turned it on, then walked to the office and tapped on the door.

"Come in."

Sophie sat at the desk, frowning at the screen on her laptop when he entered.

"I'm sorry to interrupt. I finished the dishes, and the kids are asleep. Do you need anything before I go?"

She straightened and arched her shoulders backward. "What time is it?"

"Eight forty-five. I'm sorry it's so late. It's my fault."

A yawn delayed her answer. "It's no one's fault. It is what it is. Thanks for all you did tonight."

"I was glad to do it, but you're right. We can't bribe them." He winced. "You'll probably pay for that tomorrow."

"If only that could be the biggest mistake we'll ever make." She put the event in perfect perspective. As always.

"If only." He dropped onto the sofa and stretched his legs out in front of him. "This fatigue is rough."

"I hope we adjust to it quickly. I'm getting further and further behind by the day." She looked back at the computer. "You better head home. I'm going to work for another hour or so."

"How can you even think straight?"

"Who said I was?" She looked up and gave him a silly grin.

He'd seen that grin when she'd studied late for finals or at the end of a long night at a youth event at church when they were teenagers. She was the same person on the inside. The beauty and joy that he'd loved in her then was deeper now. She tackled anything thrown at her with resolve. Yes, a calculated resolve that involved lists and planning, but she never backed away from a challenge or project.

The girl he'd loved had become an amazing woman. If anything had changed, it was only that her heart had grown bigger. He'd never be sorry that he'd loved her. Knowing her, loving her, had been worth the pain of losing her. He couldn't imagine taking on these kids with anyone else.

"Kevin?"

He pushed the thoughts away. How long had he been staring at her?

"I'm sorry. See, I can't think straight, either." He

stood and headed for the door. "I'll see you in the morning." He resisted the urge to touch her shoulder as he passed her chair on his way out of the office and waved instead. "Good night."

He sat in his truck for a long time with his head resting against the steering wheel.

Sophie was beautiful. He couldn't deny it. Her spirit and sweetness amazed him.

The part of him that had fallen for her years ago still appreciated her attributes.

And the shattered heart she'd left him with still bore the scars of her rejection. He had to remind himself—daily, if necessary—that the love and compassion she lavished on the children would never be his.

He swallowed the pain that rose up from his callous soul and drove himself home. Away from the warmth of the family that belonged to him. Well, part of them belonged to him.

Chapter Seven

By Friday afternoon Sophie had found her rhythm with the kids, but the idea of having Kevin's help on Saturday morning was the main thought that kept her going through the day. A week of being up early and dressed every morning before Kevin arrived, along with never being able to relax, had taken its toll. She was ready for a day without the full responsibility on her.

It seemed like ages since she'd awakened in her loft, made a cup of whatever kind of caffeine she wanted and stared out the giant wall of windows to gather her thoughts before her day truly began.

"Soapy, I wanna cookie." Jade stood at the door of Sophie's room, a confirmation that quiet times were to be treasured and rare now. A delightful confirmation—because she was a precious child—but a reminder, nonetheless.

"After dinner, sweetie." She brushed her hair and shook it loose around her shoulders. It was nice not to have it in the ponytail for a change. "Uncle K will be here soon." She'd changed into a teal shirt with tiny buttons and jeans. The full-length mirror she'd propped against the wall in the far corner of the room reflected her efforts. Feminine, and not over-the-top.

Not bad. Not your best, but not awful.

She looked down at her toes. "Jade, we need pedicures."

"Pet what?" Her little brow wrinkled.

"We need to paint our toenails." Sophie scooped her up and carried her down the hall, tickling her tummy all along the way. "Purple for you and red for me."

Jade giggled and pushed Sophie's hands away. "I want pink. Bubblegum pink like Mommy did."

Sophie cringed inside, hoping this innocent conversation didn't take a turn to sadness. She made every effort to keep her tone normal. "Bubblegum pink it is."

"Yay!" Jade wiggled her tiny hands close to Sophie's face. "Fingers, too."

Relief that Jade had enjoyed the moment without sorrow flooded Sophie.

"Fingers, too." She grabbed Jade's hand and pretended to nibble on her fingers. "I'm gonna gobble you up."

Jade squealed and ran away when Sophie lowered her to the living room floor.

"What about you, Carter?" She leaned over the edge of his multipaneled play yard and tousled his hair. The flexible setup allowed her to see Carter while she worked in the kitchen or did chores. She'd added several toys to keep him occupied before she'd stepped down the hall to change clothes.

Sophie didn't ask herself why she'd wanted to change. Maybe it was the remains of Carter's lunch on her college tee or the dried yogurt on her jeans that Jade had smeared there while she ate her afternoon snack.

No. She hadn't changed because Kevin was on his way. She'd done it for herself.

He probably wouldn't notice anyway.

"Ball." Carter tossed a fabric-covered ball across his space and laughed. He quickly crawled to retrieve it and tossed it again, content to play on his own for the moment.

Sophie heard the key in the front door and pulled her hair over one shoulder. She suddenly didn't know where to stand or what to do with her hands.

You're being silly. Stop it. It's not like he's coming to see you. Or like you'd even want him to. This is Kevin. Remember that.

Carter tossed a ball out of the play yard, and it landed at her feet. She stooped to retrieve it as Kevin came in.

Jade ran to wrap her arms around his legs.

"Hey, there." He picked her up and kissed the top of her head. "Have you been a good girl today?"

"Soapy's gonna pet my toenails."

Sophie caught the glint in his eyes when he tried not to laugh at Jade.

"Is she? Is that a new way to play the piggy game?" He tucked his lips between his teeth and waited for Jade to answer.

"No, silly. With bubble gum."

"The piggies want bubble gum?" It was fun to see his natural interaction with Jade. He was as authentic as the uniform he wore. Khaki pants and a green polo shirt with his store logo. Kevin Lane embraced life and all it threw at him. And he was doing it with a lightheartedness she envied.

"You're silly." Jade's giggles made Sophie smile.

"I'm not going to pet your toenails, Jade. I'm going to paint them. It's a pedicure."

Jade grabbed Kevin's face in her hands and pulled it even with hers. "See, Uncle K. I told you. She's gonna pet my toenails."

"Okay, then." He winked at Jade and set her down. "Hey, Carter. Can I have a hug?"

Carter pushed himself to his feet and toddled across the width of the play space. He maneuvered through, and sometimes stepped on, the toys inside. He was adorable. Round cheeks and wisps of blond hair showcased his blue eyes. That boy was going to be a handsome man one day.

Kevin picked him up and tossed him in the air. "Look out. You're going higher next time." He caught Carter and tossed him up again.

"Me and Rosie, too!" Jade came running across the room with her doll.

"Looks like you've got your hands full. I'm going to get to work. I'll be in the office if you need me."

"Sure." He picked up Carter and waved the boy's hand. "Say 'Bye, Soapy.'"

"Bye-bye." Carter blew her a kiss.

Sophie closed the door and leaned against it. After a deep breath and a self-scolding reminder that Kevin was her fiancé in name only, she sat at the desk and opened her computer.

Domesticity must mess with mental faculties. In the years since she and Kevin had separated, she'd never thought of him romantically again.

Well, not often, and never with any conscious acceptance of the idea.

Now, after spending every morning and night in his

company and working together to provide a home life for the kids, her mind betrayed her with thoughts of what it would be like if the fantasy were real. If she and Kevin were truly a couple and not just co-parents.

Fatigue was getting to her.

Playing house was for kids. She was a grown woman. It was time to expel the wayward thoughts from her mind before they had time to take root and cause real problems. Like an awkwardness whenever Kevin was around.

Lord, I'm too tired for this. Taxes wait for no one. I need to focus on my work and not on some ideal that's popped into my weary brain.

No matter how appealing the fantasy seemed, it was destined to be short-lived.

"I wondered if you were coming out of there tonight." Kevin looked up from the book he was reading to Jade and Carter.

"Soapy, sit by me." Jade patted the cushion on the sectional and snuggled closer to him.

Sophie looked reluctant at first, but she joined them and pulled Carter into her lap when he reached out both hands and grunted.

Twenty minutes later the kids were tucked into their beds. He turned on the night-light in Carter's room and closed the door.

In the living area, he found Sophie making one of her flavored coffees. "What's the flavor of the night?" He settled on a stool at the island and watched her back as she pulled a mug from the cabinet over her fancy coffee machine.

She held the cabinet door open and glanced over her shoulder. "Chocolate raspberry. Do you want a cup?"

"That's not a real flavor."

"Oh, it's a real flavor. You're going to love it." She grabbed another mug for him and set it on the counter. After a few quick pushes, the machine gave a long beep and groaned to life.

"It's great with shortbread cookies."

"How can you eat like that?" He waved off the cookie she offered. "I'm active every day and struggle to keep my activity level high enough to burn off what I eat."

"Stress eating is a thing. I'm sure I'll relax soon enough, but tonight I'm having chocolate raspberry coffee and a shortbread cookie. Or two."

"In that case, I'll take one, too." He reached across the island for the package of cookies.

Sophie poured their coffee and sat beside him. "Tomorrow should be easier for both of us."

"Not for me." He popped the rest of the cookie into his mouth.

"Why not?"

"The Gran Colina Expo is tomorrow."

Her eyes grew wide. "The expo?"

"Yes. It's this same weekend every year. The store always does a big booth."

"I know the expo is tomorrow, but I didn't know you were going there instead of being here." Her voice tightened with every word in spite of her obvious attempts to keep it calm.

"I told you about it the other day."

She broke the rest of her cookie into tiny bits. "I didn't hear you say you wouldn't be here."

He shrugged. "I don't know if I said that, but vendors

from all over the area are hosting. It's one of my biggest promo events of the year. It's January. People are starting to think about the spring. Hiking, fishing, all those outdoor things. I go so I can sell them everything they need for that. It's a huge deal for my company. I thought you knew."

"Why would I just know?" She took the napkin covered in cookie crumbs and tossed it into the trash. She kept her back to him and leaned on the counter with her head down. Her hair hung forward, hiding her face.

He took his mug to the sink. "I'm sorry, Sophie. I can't miss it."

"We need to coordinate our schedules." She didn't look up even though he stood right beside her. "They need us. Both of us."

"I've been here, Sophie. Morning and night."

"Well, I've been here all day and all night. Every day and every night. I need to know when you've got extra things on your schedule."

He lifted a hand and pushed her hair over her shoulder. "Okay. We can set up an online calendar. That way we'll both know what the other has coming up." He let his hand rest on her shoulder and fingered her silky hair.

She sniffed. "Fine."

She said it, but he knew she didn't mean it. If ever there was a misused word, *fine* was it.

Kevin leaned closer. "Tell me what's wrong."

"I can't."

"Please." He gently tugged on the strands of hair he held. "I'm a good listener."

"It seems petty."

He turned her toward him and put a hand on each shoulder, then leaned in to look her in the eye. "There's nothing petty about you, Sophie Owens. Never has been."

She wrapped her arms around her middle. "It's little things. I miss working on my laptop at Cup o' Caff with a hot latte. I forgot how much I enjoy that. Don't misunderstand. I love Jade and Carter, but I have no privacy. I can't even make a phone call alone. You'd be surprised how busy those two can be. They're everywhere all at once. They're adorable. I love them, but they're everywhere. And noisy. So noisy." She dropped her head again. "I sound so selfish. I really do love them. You probably think I'm awful."

"I get it. You love them." He chuckled. "I don't think you're awful."

"I feel awful." Her shoulders jerked with a sob, and he pulled her head against his shoulder. She fisted the front of his shirt in her fingers and cried.

Sophie's strength amazed him. It took a lot to get to her, but staring down motherhood without a warning could unnerve anyone. This vulnerable side of her broke his heart. He wrapped his arms around her.

"I won't go to the expo. I'll call Chad. The staff can handle everything tomorrow."

She shook her head against his shirt. "It's important. I'll be fine."

There was that word again.

"You need to be more than fine."

"But you said it's the biggest event of the year." She lifted her face to him.

He wanted to kiss away the remnants of her tears. He slid his hands up her neck and held her face in his palms. Her lips parted, and she drew in the softest breath.

He couldn't do this. They were committed to each

other for the sake of the kids. If he kissed her their relationship would be forever changed. He remembered kissing her. And loving her with every ounce of his being.

His eyes searched hers. He saw no rejection there, but apprehension started to ripple the rich brown depths. At the same time, she leaned ever so slightly toward him.

He dropped his hands and backed away. "I'm sorry. I shouldn't—"

"No, you didn't. We didn't." Sophie tucked her hair behind her ears and wiped the tears from her cheeks. "And we can't." She shook her head.

"No. We can't." He pushed his hands deep into his pockets. "About tomorrow."

"I'll call my mom. She'll probably come and hang out with us if I ask her." She took another step away from him and looked at the kitchen window and then the island. "I need to, um, do some more work. Thanks for playing with the kids earlier."

"You'll call if your mom can't come?" He picked up his keys from the island.

She nodded and looked right at him without meeting his eye. "Sure. If you promise not to come by in the morning but go straight to the expo."

"I promise." He'd really messed up. "I'm sorry, Soph. I really am."

She held up one hand to stop him. "Don't, Kevin. You don't need to say anything."

"I do. We haven't been this awkward with one another since…well, since we broke up. We have to clear the air."

"Clear the air." She tightened her lips together. "Here goes. We got too close. You were being kind, and we both got carried away with the emotions of the moment. We won't let it happen again. Clear enough?"

"Very clear." He met her gaze then. "So, we're all right? No hard feelings? Nothing awkward?"

"Nothing awkward. Except you standing there continuing to talk about it." She reached out, pinched the fabric of his sleeve between two fingers and tugged him toward the door. "Good night." Both words rang with sarcasm.

He laughed at her. "Gotcha. Good night."

Kevin stood on the porch until he heard her lock the door behind him. He had only one thought on his mind as he walked to his truck.

She'd said *both*. They *both* got carried away. Part of her had wanted to kiss him back.

Chapter Eight

"Here we go." Sophie closed the back of the SUV and grabbed the handles on the double stroller. "Are you guys ready to see what's inside?"

"I want a toy." Jade sat with her feet crossed at the ankles and Rosie in her lap. Carter was strapped in beside her.

Sophie's mom laughed. "You do?"

"Yep. Carter does, too. 'Cause he's little and don't have as many toys as me."

"That's very sweet, Jade. We'll see what they have." Sophie pushed the stroller across the uneven ground surrounding the Gran Colina Community Center.

"This is a good idea. I didn't think we'd make it to the expo this year." Diane walked with Sophie toward the entrance. "I want to see what they have in the library booth."

"We need a day out. Thanks for coming. We'd have been stuck at the house without your help."

Diane adjusted the canopy on Carter's side of the stroller. "You seem to be taking everything in stride.

Honestly, I wasn't sure how this was going to work. I've been praying for you. And for Kevin. Two kids is a lot."

"We're handling it. Don't quit praying, but don't worry about us." Sophie maneuvered the stroller through the wide front entrance and followed the growing crowd into the main exhibit area.

"Look! Balloons!" Jade squealed her delight and held her hand out, opening and closing her fist. "I want pink."

Sophie laughed. "Of course, you do." They stopped at the balloon vendor and got pink for Jade and green for Carter. Diane tied the balloons to their respective seats so they could see and touch the strings of the balloons without losing them.

"Rosie wants one, too." Jade pouted a bit.

Sophie looked at her mom and back to Jade. "I have to save some money in case we find a toy for you and Carter. You can share your balloon with Rosie. I think she likes pink, too." Every conversation was a decision with kids. Endless opportunities to mess up appeared without warning. Her prayers now included a constant plea for God's help to parent the children the way Logan and Caitlyn would want.

Diane gave her a smile of approval. "You're doing fine."

"I'm doing my best and praying that's enough. More than ever I appreciate all you did for me."

Sophie turned the stroller to the left. The exhibits were set up against the outside wall and in the center of the open space. "Let's see what's on this side."

A half hour later the kids each held a new homemade toy in their lap. Carter had a stuffed horse with floppy legs and a cowboy hat. Jade cuddled a new doll. She'd insisted Rosie needed a little sister. "Rosie's the big sister. Like me."

"Wow. I didn't expect to see you guys today." Kevin's voice came from behind Sophie.

She tensed, then forced herself to relax. Her mother would notice any awkwardness between them. "We thought we'd surprise you." She felt the heat in her face when she turned and their eyes met.

He sent her an encouraging smile as he approached them in front of a booth filled with homemade jams. "You did." He crouched in front of the stroller. "What have you got there, Carter?"

Carter held the horse by its back and made it buck across his lap. "Wee. Wee."

"Ride 'em, cowboy." Kevin tugged on Carter's foot where it stuck straight out in front of the stroller. "It's a good thing you wore your boots today. Horses like a cowboy with boots."

"I gots a dolly." Jade stuck her new doll out for Kevin's inspection.

"She's almost as pretty as you and Rosie. What's her name?"

"Sissy." She tucked the new doll back into the stroller beside Rosie.

Kevin stood. "Hi, Diane. Thanks for helping Sophie today. This expo is a big deal for my company. I've never missed one."

"I always enjoy the expo. I'm glad Sophie invited me to come with her."

Kevin cut his eyes to Sophie. She gave a small shrug. "I thought it could be fun."

"I'm glad you came." He smiled at her. A full smile

that reinforced the truth of his words and his effort to keep things normal between them.

"Hi." Jackson and his wife, Allison, walked up to their group. "It's good to see the new family out together."

"Hi, Sophie." Allison wrapped her in a kind hug. She whispered, "I've been praying for you," then released her. "Did you see the cotton candy in the back corner on the other side of the exhibits? It's my weakness."

Sophie cringed and laughed at the same time. "Thanks for the warning. We may have to miss that part." She pointed at the children without them noticing her.

Allison put a hand over her mouth. "Oops. Sorry. We don't have kids yet, so I forget to be quiet sometimes."

She waved off Allison's apology. "Believe me, I'm learning, too."

Jackson and Kevin had stepped a few feet away and were talking quietly. Hopefully, nothing else had come up about the kids. She didn't have a lot of experience with lawyers, but living in her newly inverted world gave her reason for more than her customary caution— a caution Kevin thought was overdone. The longer she lived, the more she drew comfort from avoiding unnecessary risk.

Diane put a hand on her arm. "I see the library booth up on the right. I'm going to go ahead while you visit."

"We'll catch up to you soon."

Allison smiled her goodbye to Diane. "Your mother is the sweetest thing. I always try to get in her line at the bank."

"I don't know what we'd have done without her these last few weeks."

"She must be so excited about the wedding. My mom

was so happy when Jackson and I got engaged that you'd have thought it was her wedding all over again."

Allison was being kind, but the last few days, shut away from the world while she dealt with her newfound motherhood, hadn't given Sophie time to think about the temporary engagement. Of course, everyone would expect them to be planning a wedding.

She took a deep breath and prepared herself to plunge into the explanations she and Kevin had agreed to. "How sweet. That must have been a lot of fun for you and your mom."

"It was. You're going to have such a good time. If you need any suggestions on caterers or photographers, anything at all about the wedding, just shoot me a text. I'm happy to share."

"Thanks, but we've decided to wait." She patted the canopy on the stroller. "We're focusing on getting these two settled. That's taking up all of our time and energy."

Kevin and Jackson rejoined them as she finished sharing her reasons.

Allison reached out and took her hand. "I'm so sorry. I should have realized. I'm such a talker. It's okay to stop me when I'm going on and on about the wrong thing. Jackson has to do it all the time." She gave a nervous laugh. "Don't you, Jackson?"

Jackson put his arm around his wife's shoulders. "I try." He pulled her close and kissed her temple. "I'm not always successful, but I do try."

Sophie didn't want her to feel bad. "It's fine. Really."

Kevin took her hand. The suddenness surprised her until she realized his actions were for Jackson and Allison's sake. "I have to get back to my booth. Make sure you and the kids stop by before you leave." He gave her hand a gentle squeeze, then waved at Jackson and Allison as he walked away. "We'll see you tomorrow in class."

"Yes. Tomorrow." Sophie smiled at them.

"Bye." Allison wiggled her fingers at Jade and Carter. "Bye to you, too."

Sophie took a deep breath when they left her in the middle of the aisle between the exhibits. She'd survived her first social encounter, outside of church, with Kevin and mutual friends. The first outing with the kids was going well.

She'd even dealt with the wedding that would never be.

Her heart seemed a little lighter for having crossed so many bridges in one morning.

Today was a turning point. One she was glad to have behind her.

Chad pointed down the wide aisle of the expo. "Looks like you've got company."

Sophie pushed the stroller toward his booth as if she didn't have a care in the world. With her hair in a messy bun, jeans and a light jacket, she gave the appearance of an experienced mother.

"Yeah. I saw them earlier." He spoke to Chad, keeping his eyes on Sophie and the kids. His family. He had a family, complete with toys, balloons and smiles. How many times had he dreamed of that life with Sophie and their own kids? She had seen him as a daring, irresponsible teenager. Nothing he tried back then could erase that perception from her mind. Now he had her. And the kids he'd dreamed of. Only it wasn't real.

Chad bumped his arm. "Hey. Did you hear me?"

"What?" He crammed his memories away and focused on whatever he'd missed.

"I said that you're a blessed man. A fiancée like Sophie? Most men don't even aim that high. And she's great for those kids." Chad chuckled. "Logan and Caitlyn probably knew they'd need at least one grown-up for a guardian."

And there it was, wrapped in humor. The truth. People saw Kevin as a carefree adventurer. Why didn't they see the hard work he'd put into building a successful business or his commitment to God and the Gran Colina Church?

Did anyone take him seriously?

He tried not to let the sting of Chad's remarks show. "Ha. Ha. Aren't you a funny guy?"

"It's part of my charm."

"Charm. Is that what the ladies are calling it these days?" Retaliating with a playful barb was the only response that wouldn't have Kevin answering serious questions from Chad.

Kevin didn't have the heart to be upset with Chad. Everyone in Gran Colina had known each other forever. He and Chad had laughed and teased each other since elementary school. The remark wasn't intended to be disrespectful or mean. If Chad knew how it hurt, he'd feel terrible. Kevin's feelings weren't Chad's responsibility.

Getting beyond the reputation as a man who played games for a living and being validated as a businessman was Kevin's job. If only he could figure out how to do it.

The woman and two small children coming his way made the need more urgent.

"You must have become quite the charmer. How else did you get Sophie to agree to marry you?"

A crashing sound caught their attention. Two little boys were standing in the middle of a sea of basketballs they'd knocked off one of the displays.

"Sorry!" Both boys laughed and ran in the opposite direction.

"I got it, boss. You go see your lady."

Chad motioned for another of the employees to help clean up the basketballs, while Kevin stepped into the aisle to greet Sophie and the kids.

These three people had turned his world upside down. Having them in it presented new emotions and an excitement he hadn't noticed was building in his soul.

A deep joy at knowing he had an opportunity to make a difference in Jade's and Carter's lives made him wonder if God intended to use his new circumstances as a way to change the way people looked at him.

He would care for them because he loved them. Would a change in his public persona be a side effect of that responsibility?

He prayed so.

"How's the booth doing?" Sophie's cheeks were pinker than usual, no doubt because of last night's close encounter.

In an effort to put her at ease, he pointed at the basketballs all over the floor. "Better than it looks at the moment."

"Well, it can't all be fun and games." As soon as the words were out of her mouth he saw her eyes light up with their double meaning. "Or can it?"

"Touché."

He peeked into the stroller and found both kids asleep. "Well done."

"I let them play on the obstacle course on the other side of the expo. They loved it."

"Is your mom having a good time?" He didn't know what to do with his hands. His arms started to feel the itch of a man about to break out in hives. Although he'd worried she might not be able to relax around him, he was the one with the problem. He rubbed his forearms and worried as beads of sweat trickled down the back of his neck.

Sophie grabbed his hands and leaned in close. "Relax. We're okay. You're okay." She spoke softly and smiled at him.

No one could read him like Sophie. He took a deep breath. "You're right."

"Is this a private conversation, or can anyone listen in?" Chad surprised them both when he spoke behind Kevin.

Sophie dropped her hands. "Hi, Chad. I see you're on cleanup today. Be honest, did you make the mess?"

"Who, me?" Chad teased her back with a grin.

A green-eyed emotion crawled up the back of Kevin's neck, and he clinched his fists. Jealousy? Where had that come from?

"You were probably competing to see who could stack them the highest, right?" Sophie included them both in her smile, but her gaze settled on Kevin. "You won, didn't you?"

Relief flooded through Kevin. Sophie had managed to deter Chad from his obvious teasing about the two of them whispering together and holding hands, and at the same time let Kevin know by her attention that she wasn't interested in flirting with Chad.

Not that she'd ever flirted with anyone. Even in their youth, her interactions were always sincere, never misleading.

Two men from the Gran Colina Park and Recreation Department approached. Kevin touched Sophie on the arm. "You'll have to excuse me. I have some information these gentlemen need."

"Go ahead. I'm meeting Mom at the entrance. I just wanted to see your booth and let you know we're going home."

"I'll be there as soon as I finish here. It may be late, but I'll try to make it in time to put the kids to bed." He looked over his shoulder and saw Chad chatting with the men. "I really need to go. They're some of my biggest customers." He started to walk away.

"Oh, just a sec."

"What is it?"

"What did Jackson say to you earlier?"

In his peripheral vision, he caught Chad waving him over. "He wants to talk to us about the home inspection. He's sending us an email this afternoon with the details. We'll talk about it tonight."

"Okay." She turned the stroller toward the entrance. "I'll see you at home."

He watched her for a moment before he heard Chad call his name. "Do you have the proposal for the rec department?"

"Yeah. It's in my computer bag." He dug out the paperwork that represented the largest part of his annual business and got his head in the game. The game just happened to be his livelihood.

Kevin handled Adventure Lane Sports with his full attention. That's how it had grown to be the biggest independent sporting goods store in a fifty-mile radius.

The success became more important than ever as he

watched the three people who counted on him leave the expo. He wouldn't let them down.

The clock on the dash of his truck read eight thirty when Kevin pulled into the driveway that night. Sophie's earlier text warned him that the kids were asleep and asked him to join her in the office when he arrived.

He grabbed a bottle of water from the refrigerator, then rapped his knuckles on the open door. "Can I come in?"

"Sure." She sat cross-legged on the end of the sofa with her laptop. "I'm just reading the forms Jackson sent."

"I took a look at them during a lull this afternoon. I didn't see anything that will be an issue for us. Did you?" He sat on the opposite end of the sofa.

"No. It's just paperwork and the actual home inspection. I had a couple of questions and emailed Jackson. He doesn't think we have anything to worry about. Basically, the fact that Judge Carlisle let us keep the kids in the first place goes in our favor. The rest is a formality. The hurdles that could have been a problem, like background checks, have already been cleared." She closed the laptop and slid it onto the table at her elbow.

"Great." He hoped this inspection would seal their legal position as guardians. He wanted the paperwork behind him and Judge Carlisle out of their lives and business, so he and Sophie could live without the weight of their temporary engagement hanging over their heads.

Kevin wasn't good at pretending.

"Did you do well today at the expo?" Her question brought him back to the moment.

"It was a great day. The best ever, if I had to guess. We won't know for certain until we do the accounting." He was relieved, after having left her to deal with the kids while he worked. He hadn't wanted her sacrifice to be for nothing.

She uncurled her legs and leaned forward. "I'm really happy for you. It was nice to see you in your element."

"Since you're not very athletic and have never actually been in my store?" He grinned at her. "Not everyone can get away with not exercising."

"I exercise." Her face wrinkled in disapproval.

"What?"

"My latest sport is chasing two little ones from dawn till dark every day." Her smirk made him laugh.

"I'll give you that one." She had a healthy glow some people never achieved, but it wasn't from the kids. She'd always had it.

"I walk. My loft was so close to everything in town that I could walk to dinner or the Cup o' Caff. I usually got in several miles every day." She lifted her arm and looked at her fitness-tracking watch. "So far today, I'm on track to double the steps I took in a day before the kids became part of my routine."

"Well done, and when you need new shoes or workout clothes, please come into the store. I'll give you the fiancée's discount." Having her see a part of his success today validated his work. He was surprised at how much that meant to him. Seeing the store could elevate her opinion of him—show her his business side.

Sophie narrowed her eyes at him. "That's not a plot to get me to take over your accounting for the fiancée discount, is it? Because my walking shoes are about walked out."

Was he ready to be that vulnerable? To show her the books? If they weren't raising the kids together, he might never have considered it. But he trusted her. More than anyone. What better way was there to show her how committed he was to their long-term connection. Even after the engagement ended—and he had no doubt it would as soon as the judge retired—they'd be connected for Jade and Carter.

On a whim he decided to take the leap. "Hmm. I hadn't thought of that, but if you can improve my bottom line by lowering my accounting fees—"

She tossed a throw pillow at him. "I challenge you to find a better accountant."

"Okay, then. I'll have the office manager get in touch with you next week."

Her expression changed to concern. "Kevin, I wasn't truly asking for your business. You don't have to do that."

"Don't I? What will people think if you buy your walking shoes somewhere else and I don't use you for my accounting? I hadn't thought about it, but we need to make sure everything we do validates our new commitment."

"I hadn't considered that, either. That's just the kind of thing Judge Carlisle would notice."

"I'd also like to move some things into the guest room tomorrow after church. If they're coming next week for the home inspection, they need to see that I'm putting down roots here." He watched her for any sign of disagreement. He'd never want her to be uncomfortable.

She didn't miss a beat. "Would you mind doing it while the kids nap? I can put them down after lunch.

Then I could get in a couple of hours in the office if you can watch them after they wake up in the afternoon."

"That's good for me." He stifled a yawn. "I think I'll head home. I'm exhausted."

"There's no guarantee that feeling will go away before Carter graduates from high school."

"What about those teenage years when we won't be able to drag them out of bed in the mornings? Can't we sleep then?"

They both laughed and walked to the front door.

Her relaxed conversation made him grateful that she'd moved beyond his near kiss. Being able to tease with her was natural. He was glad they hadn't messed that up with a kiss they'd have both regretted.

She pulled the sleeves of her shirt over her hands and held them together. "I guess we'll see you in the morning."

"I'll be here." He unlocked the door. "Doughnuts?"

"Not tomorrow. Toast and scrambled eggs. They had enough treats today."

"See, you're already a good mom." He reached for the knob. "I'll be here by eight."

"Mommy!" Jade's cry went through him like electricity.

Kevin followed Sophie as she hurried down the hall.

"I want Mommy!" Jade flailed, and her arms tangled in the sheets. Sophie eased herself onto the floor beside her bed.

Kevin stood in the doorway holding his breath and saying a silent prayer. Jade's outburst broke his heart for the little girl.

"I'm here, Jade. It's me, Soapy." She wrapped Jade in her arms and pulled the child to her chest.

Carter cried from the other room. "I'll get him." Kevin picked up the boy and swayed back and forth in an effort to soothe him.

"Mommy." Carter's cries were muted compared to Jade's, and he whimpered his way back to sleep in a couple of minutes.

Kevin laid him in the crib and pulled the dinosaur quilt up to his tiny shoulders. He eased the door shut and went back to Jade's room.

Sophie sat on the floor by Jade's bed, humming and rocking the sleepy girl in her arms. She shushed him silently and waved him out of the room.

He left reluctantly. He wanted to help, but Jade was settled against Sophie, and any interruption from him could cause the child to become upset all over again.

Ten minutes later he sat in Logan's chair, having prayed everything he knew to pray over the children. Sophie came into the living area and collapsed onto the sectional.

"How often does this happen?" Kevin had no idea she'd been dealing with tantrums in the night. When he'd stayed at the house for the week after Logan and Caitlyn passed, Jade had wandered into their room in a sleepy stupor, but she hadn't screeched out in her sleep and become hysterical.

Sophie didn't answer him.

"Every night?"

"Pretty much." She shrugged. "They're missing them so much and don't know what to think about them being gone." Every word echoed with sorrow.

"How do you manage both of them at once?"

She turned her palms up in surrender. "We all pile up in my bed and cry together."

The brutal honesty of the confession made his heart ache.

"What can I do, Sophie? I feel helpless and like you're carrying the lion's share of the responsibility."

"I don't know that there's anything anyone can do at this point. It's going to take time. I tell them that Mommy and Daddy are with Jesus. Then Jade wants to drive to the church and look at the pictures of Jesus in her class."

"Oh, Sophie. I'm so sorry for them. And for you." He moved from the chair to sit on the ottoman in front of her.

Kevin didn't know how to help her, so he did the thing he always did when he was without answers. He turned to Jesus. He took her hand in both of his and prayed with her. The words tumbled from him as he asked God for help and peace for the children. Then he asked for strength for Sophie and wisdom for both of them.

She echoed his amen.

"Thank you, Kevin. I miss Caitlyn so much it hurts. I can't imagine how the kids feel."

"I know. Logan is the person I'd call for help on a night like tonight." He doubted he'd ever have a truer friend.

"We're lost without our best friends." Her tone was hollow with pain.

A flicker of an idea whispered to his heart. "That's what we need."

"What?" Her moist eyes narrowed in confusion.

"We're missing our best friends—the people we turned to for help and wisdom. Our sounding boards, the people who told us when we had a stupid idea or needed to be patient or pushed us when we were stuck."

Her brow furrowed. "That's what we don't have. What are you saying we need?"

It might sound off-the-wall to her, but he had to put it out there. "We need a best friend. A person who'll listen and take our problems as seriously as we do. Someone to prop us up when we're faltering and hold us back when we're heading into danger."

"I don't have another friend like that." Her shoulders slumped lower than ever.

He tugged on the hand he still held. "You do." He'd make the offer. Surely, she'd see it as a genuine solution to help them both through their grief.

She lifted her eyes to his, and he saw a glimmer of hope in their depths.

"Me. I'll be your best friend, and you'll be mine. We promised to be there for the kids, knowing it meant we'd be together for their sakes. We didn't realize—at least I didn't—how much we'd need another adult."

Sophie didn't say anything, so he continued, "No one else has a clue about what we're dealing with. There's no one who understands what is, and isn't, happening between you and me. It's perfectly logical." He tilted his head to one side. "You, the master of all lists, see the truth of what I'm proposing, don't you?"

"You're proposing again?" She laughed, a little snicker, at first, which grew into a genuine laugh. "You're the only person who's ever proposed to me. Now you've done it again even though we're already engaged."

Years ago, he'd never have imagined she'd laugh at the idea of his proposal. At least she wasn't telling him to leave and come back tomorrow when he wasn't so tired he couldn't think straight.

"I hear you laughing, but it's what we need." She sobered, and he continued "I'm proposing friendship for Sophie Owens. And I'm asking for her to be my best friend. I'm sorry I didn't understand how important we'd be to each other when we first got into this. We've been trying to muddle through by working out schedules and chores, but we need more than that. We need support and caring. Comfort and a safe place to vent."

"That's exactly what I need. How did you know?" Her face relaxed in relief, and she took a deep breath.

"Because it's what I need, too. This is hard, Sophie. Harder than anything most people will ever face in their lifetime. I'm brave, but sometimes I need help."

Saying the words aloud hit him deep in the middle of his chest. How many times had he put on a brave face and taken on an adventure or challenge without letting anyone see how much it took out of him?

So often that no one realized the depth of his pain.

She deserved his total honesty. "Raising kids is tough. I'm scared. More scared than I've ever been in my life." Except when she broke up with him and he'd had to learn to live and breathe without her. The one person who'd almost destroyed him by walking away was tied to him forever. It took every ounce of his courage to say his next words. "I can't do it without you."

"But you're always so brave."

"People only see my adventurous spirit. They don't see beyond that to the real me. The real me gets as scared as the next guy. I just don't ever talk about it. To anyone. I need a friend."

Had she nodded her head? The slight movement may

or may not be agreement. The deliberate nod that followed removed his doubt.

"I'm in." She clasped her other hand over his. "I need you, too."

She needed him.

A rumbling in his soul awakened a long-dormant love for her. The strength of it frightened him, but he would never back away from her again. No matter what she said.

"I'm in, too."

God, help me. I think I'm falling in love with Sophie all over again.

And I can never let her know.

Chapter Nine

Sophie scanned the living area again. "What do you think?"

Kevin stood by the kitchen island and watched the kids eat their snack. "I think you're too worried." He seemed overly casual while her nerves were wound tight.

"Maybe you're not worried enough." She fluffed the pillows on the sectional and opened the blinds to let in more of the afternoon sun. "When Jackson called to say the home inspection was this afternoon, he didn't know why they'd moved it up from Friday."

"It's Wednesday. They only moved it up two days." He grinned at her. "My guess is they're trying to catch you with dust under the rug or a dirty dish in the sink. It'll all be over if there's a toy on the sofa or laundry in the basket."

She glared at him. "You're not helping." This was one of those times when she thought he didn't take things as seriously as he should. You couldn't just blow off a home inspection like it was no big deal.

"I am helping. That's why I took today off—to help you prepare."

"You're required to be here. They can't inspect you if you're not."

"No one is going to inspect me." He laughed and turned his head to look at her from the corner of his eye.

She tried not to laugh. "You're so irritating." His lighthearted approach to most of life was infuriating. And sometimes funny.

"Thank you." He wiped milk from Carter's chin and took him out of the high chair. "Go get Soapy." He set the boy down and gave him a nudge in her direction.

Chubby cheeks and a toddling gait were irresistible. She scooped him up and gave him a hug. "Uncle K isn't playing fair."

Kevin cleared his throat. "I'm reminding you that you're stressing. And stressing isn't good or necessary. Relax. Jackson said everything is in order, and we don't need to worry."

She put Carter in his play yard and dumped a basket with several of his favorite toys in with him. "Here you go, big guy. Have fun."

"That's better. The investigator needs to see life as normal, which means laundry, dishes and noise. Anything else isn't real."

The doorbell rang, and Jade slid off her stool. "Who is it?" She ran to catch Sophie, who took a deep breath and opened the door.

"Hi, I'm Mrs. Young."

"Hello." Jade greeted the woman in perfect hostess mode. "We're having snacks. Do you want a cookie? Soapy tried to make 'em, but Uncle K had to help." She reached up, took the court investigator's hand and pulled her into the house. Then she held her other hand close to her mouth in an effort to hide her next words from Sophie. "Soapy's not a good cooker."

"Is that so?" The woman smiled at Kevin and Sophie, then followed Jade to the kitchen island.

An hour later, after the investigator left, Sophie closed the front door and turned to Kevin. "Well, if real is what they wanted, they should be satisfied."

She looked down at her shirt. Carter's apple juice covered her right side.

"Who knew the kids would be the center of attention the entire time?" Kevin tossed her a kitchen towel.

She blotted the dampness and gave up. "I'm going to change." A sopping mess in less than an hour hadn't been the impression she'd hoped to make on Mrs. Young.

He caught her elbow when she headed toward the hallway. "We passed. That's the biggest hurdle, and it's behind us." Apparently, he'd been more tense than he'd let on, because his countenance relaxed. She couldn't shift emotional gears as quickly or easily as he did.

"Yes." She nodded. "I'm relieved, but my nerves need to catch up with the results. I was on edge the whole time, worried she'd ask more about the engagement and our plans—or lack of plans—to marry."

"The way you answered her was perfect. Putting the kids first is the truth. She could see your sincerity."

"Phew, I'm glad." She huffed out a breath. "I'll be right back."

"I'm going to start our celebratory dinner. You're gonna love it. Tacos."

"Yay!" Jade swung Rosie and Sissy in circles on the rug in the center of the living area. "Tacos!"

Sophie smiled at him. "Uncle K for the win."

She walked down the hall thinking how true that

was. Kevin had been a great help in getting ready for the inspection. Having him at the house to prepare—and during the actual appointment—had eased some of her anxiety.

He really was a true friend.

Had she held his lifestyle against him unfairly? The way he handled responsibility for the kids, the legal process of guardianship and even his business made it more apparent with each passing day that underneath the fun exterior lived a man of great character.

And heart. A heart that used to be hers.

On Friday Jackson called to tell them that the inspection report had been delivered to the judge, and everything was fine. The next court date was fast approaching. Another thing checked off her list added to Sophie's peace of mind.

She had a chicken in the electric pressure cooker when Kevin came home.

Home? When had she started to think of this house as Kevin's home? It was not something she was ready to ponder.

"Hi." She busied herself wiping the kitchen counter to keep from looking at him. The heat in her cheeks warned her they were pink.

"Hello. What's up, guys?"

She watched the kids dash into his outstretched arms. They weren't born to him, but he had made them his own in the weeks since Logan and Caitlyn had passed. Her heart warmed at the sight of him tickling and hugging them.

Jade grabbed Kevin's hand. "Uncle K, Soapy is cooking." Her whisper made him laugh.

"She's not supposed to cook, is she?" He slowly moved his head back and forth as he spoke.

Jade matched his head movement like a tiny pendulum. "No." She dragged the word out. "You're the cooker."

They enjoyed their constant joking about her culinary deficiencies. Most of it was true. Her skills were basic, and the results were often inedible. She kept trying because she was certain motherhood required her to.

"Hey. I can cook." Sophie tossed the dishcloth onto the counter and hurried around the sofa. "And I can tickle, too."

She grabbed up Carter and blew on his tummy. His answering squeal started a tickle war that lasted for several minutes.

Breathless, in a heap on the floor, the kids begged for mercy, and Sophie returned to the kitchen.

Kevin joined her while the kids busied themselves with toys. "How did things go today?"

"Good. It's getting easier, or I'm getting better. I'm not sure which." She pulled a dish of yellow rice from the microwave and stirred it. The center was crunchy, but the edges were almost done. She lifted the heaping spoon to show Kevin. "But even I know that I'm not good at this." She dropped the rice back into the bowl and added more water.

"Not everyone cooks." He returned the dish to the microwave and punched in more cooking time. "Don't let it bother you."

"I hope the chicken is better than the rice. I found the recipe online. It smells good." She shrugged. She'd like nothing better than to be perfect. But if she hadn't known she'd never be that before becoming a guardian, she was sure of it now.

"It does." He pulled plates from the cabinet. "If you want a half hour in the office, I can finish dinner."

"Are you helping me to have more work time, or are you hoping to salvage the meal?"

"Hmm…do I have to answer that?"

"I think I'll spare my feelings and let you off the hook." She picked up her water glass and left him in the kitchen.

The office had quickly become her haven. She opened her laptop and started to work her accounts—until her battery died. She couldn't find her charger, then remembered that Carter had toddled into the room after his nap. He'd probably picked it up and laid it somewhere.

A cursory scan of the room revealed nothing. She opened the desk drawers that Carter could reach to see if he'd tucked it away. It was crammed into the file drawer and hung on the hanging file frame. She untangled it from the hardware and a file that had slipped between the others tore when she pulled the cord free.

She opened the file and couldn't believe her eyes.

"Kevin. You need to come in here." She'd searched everywhere for this paperwork and decided it didn't exist.

"I'm about to take the chicken out of the pot." His voice was muffled by the closed door.

She raised her voice. "Please. Come now." Her breath caught in her throat.

He opened the door. "What is it?"

"This." She held the file up for him to see. "I searched everywhere for this. I didn't even tell you that I was looking for it, because I didn't want to get your hopes up in case it didn't exist. I'd given up." The pitch of her voice rose with every word.

"What's in this mystery file?"

"The mortgage. It's insured." Tears of joy fell onto her cheeks. "The house is paid off in the event of their death. They did everything right for the kids."

He looked as shocked as she was.

Excitement bubbled up in her, and, without thinking, she threw her arms around his neck.

He lifted her off the ground. "You're serious?" He set her on her feet and sat on the corner of the desk.

She took a step away from him and tugged at the hem of her shirt, still holding the file in front of her. She couldn't do that. Leaping into his arms wasn't part of their arrangement. It would only make life harder when the judge resigned and she gave him back his ring.

He pushed his hands through his hair as he processed the information. "We won't have to take money out of the trust to pay the monthly payments?"

"No. Not one cent." Shock made her mind race. "Do you realize what the compound interest on the trust will do without making those monthly withdrawals? Even if I paid a portion of the mortgage for staying here—and I can do that, pay rent into the trust—over time, it was going to deplete a large portion of their trust."

"This is an amazing day. First the good report on the home inspection, then Jackson saying everything is on track for permanent guardianship, now the mortgage." His face was full of genuine happiness. "This is a rush. Like a zip line rush."

"Look at me. I'm Mommy."

They turned to see Jade in the doorway wearing Caitlyn's sunglasses. The large pink frames and reflective lenses almost covered her face.

"I look pretty." Her rosy lips curved upward, and she pushed the glasses higher on the bridge of her nose.

"Yes, you do." Kevin crouched down in front of her. "I can see myself in your glasses."

"Uh-uh. I can see you, but you can't see you." She turned and left the room still wearing the sunglasses.

Sophie watched her go. The sweetness of the moment would be a treasured memory for years to come. Knowing that Jade was feeling secure enough to think of her mother in happy ways comforted Sophie. As difficult as it was, she and Kevin were getting the fundamentals right. "Her world just got better, and she doesn't even know it."

Kevin stood. "I think it got better in a lot of ways. That's the first time she's played with something that belonged to Caitlyn and it didn't make her sad."

"You're right." She smiled at him. "Today is an amazing day."

"Zip line amazing?" He raised his brows.

She tucked the file into the drawer with all the paperwork she needed to finish getting Logan and Caitlyn's affairs in order.

Although it was indeed an amazing day, she still wasn't one for unnecessary risk. She never would be. "I'll take your word for it."

Kevin signed Carter into the nursery at church on Sunday morning. "You be a good boy and have fun."

He set the child on his feet and watched him hurry as fast as his legs would take him to a little girl playing in a small pool filled with plastic balls. Carter held on to the side of the pool and tried to climb in with her, only to tumble forward and land in the middle of the balls.

"Whoa." Carter pushed himself upright and tossed a ball across the room.

Jackson walked up beside Kevin and looked over his shoulder at Carter. "He seems to be adjusting well."

"I think he is. He's so young. Don't misunderstand me—he still has times where he's inconsolable—but he's going to adapt to everything quicker than Jade. Just because she's older. I do hate that he won't remember Logan and Caitlyn."

Jackson clapped a hand on Kevin's shoulder. "He'll remember. You and Sophie will make sure of it."

"We'll have to." Kevin turned away from the nursery door and faced Jackson. He didn't want Carter to see him and change his mind about being content to play with his little friend. "Thank you for all you've done about this whole situation, Jackson. Sophie and I would have been lost without your help."

As soon as Kevin said her name, she came around the corner at the end of the hall. She wore a soft pink sweater that contrasted with her dark hair. Her skirt and boots made her look like a model in a TV commercial. When she saw him, she smiled. A small acknowledgment that they belonged together. It hit him hard, and Jackson must have seen it in his face because he glanced over his shoulder and then back at Kevin.

"Is there something you want to tell me?" Jackson cut right to the point.

"About what?" Kevin feigned ignorance.

"About you and Sophie. I see that look in your eye. I'm guessing that Carter isn't the only one adjusting to the new people in his life."

Kevin shot a look at Sophie. She stood in the hallway talking to Allison. "Sophie and I are settling into our roles as guardians."

"And as a newly engaged couple?" Jackson let the question hang in the air.

"We're good." He still hadn't come to grips with the feelings that had begun to stir in his heart for Sophie. The feelings had to be dealt with, but it was something he'd keep to himself.

"After you got engaged so quickly, I was concerned for the two of you and the kids. I'm glad to see it's working out."

Because he was an officer of the court, Kevin wouldn't tell Jackson the temporary state of the engagement. It might jeopardize their case. But as his friend, Kevin appreciated the concern.

Sophie and Allison headed toward them.

"Me, too." Kevin turned to greet the ladies. "Me, too."

Allison slid her hand into Jackson's. "You're going to be late if you don't hurry."

"Yes, ma'am." Jackson tipped an imaginary hat at his wife. "We best be going then."

Kevin grinned. "For someone who's never spent a minute of his life on a horse, you sure do sound like a cowboy."

"I'll have you know, I rode a horse every Saturday morning when I was a boy." Jackson smirked.

"The one in front of the grocery store on Main Street." Allison tugged Jackson toward his classroom, and left Kevin and Sophie laughing in the hallway.

"They're hilarious." Sophie walked beside him.

"Hilarious." He spoke without thinking. His mind

was on how quickly Jackson had reacted to Kevin's expression when he'd seen Sophie.

On the one hand, it was great. He and Sophie needed people to see them as a couple. On the other hand, it troubled him. Would his budding feelings for her show on his face when he was with her?

What if she discovered he was having feelings for her before he figured out what those feelings truly were?

They'd agreed to keep their friendship *friendly*. Anything else could ruin everything they were building together for the children. He needed to get a grip on himself.

When she tucked her hand into the crook of his elbow before they entered their classroom, he knew he better do it quickly or everyone in Gran Colina would know Sophie Owens was getting under his skin.

And that he liked it.

The weather was mild after lunch, so they took the kids to the park in the middle of the town square. Kevin hadn't expected to see so many people there.

Sophie found an empty spot on the end of the block and parked the SUV. "I'll unbuckle Carter. Can you grab the stroller?"

It only took a few minutes to have the kids strapped in for a ride around the perimeter of the park.

"If you guys are good, after we take a walk, you can play on the playground." Kevin decided he was getting better at parenting.

Until Jade stuck out her bottom lip. "I wanna swing."

Carter pointed at the playground, too.

Sophie caught Kevin's eye and motioned toward the swings and slide. There was a question in her look.

Unable to interpret the question, he shrugged.

She smiled at the kids. "What if we swing first and then take a walk?"

"Yay!" Jade threw both fists up high, while Carter kicked his feet as fast as he could.

"So, we're going to swing first." Kevin tried not to be annoyed, but he'd stated how he'd like to do things, and as soon as Jade objected, Sophie came up with another option. Sophie controlled everything during the daytime hours. Was is too much to think his input should be respected?

His annoyance must have been noticeable, because she leaned in and whispered to him, "If we let them play first, they'll tire themselves out and fall asleep in the stroller. It will give you and me more time for a walk. I don't know about you, but I'm ready for a chance to stretch my legs and enjoy the fresh air."

He pursed his lips in thought. "So, do you have a purpose like that every time you make a change or suggestion?" The kids pumped their legs up and down in the stroller as he pushed them along the sidewalk. Sophie walked beside him, close enough to carry on a conversation without Jade listening in.

Sophie pondered his question. "I guess so. I mean, I do try to rationalize everything." She winced. "That's just how I think. I shouldn't have said anything. We can walk first."

It was his turn to think about what she said. When they neared the gate that surrounded the playground equipment, he slowed the stroller.

"I think this is an example of putting up a united front like you mentioned. We need to back one another up when we say something. It will help them not to be confused by getting different messages from either of us."

"So, they won't be able to play one against the other, huh?" She chuckled.

"Not even."

"You're right. I should have thought of it like that. I've noticed that Jade is trying to get her way about a lot of things. While I feel sorry for her, I don't think it's good to let her manipulate us."

He was glad Sophie understood his perspective. "Exactly. We've got a lifetime of parenting ahead of us. If we don't take the reins now, only God knows what future problems we could have." He pushed the stroller through the playground entrance.

Sophie pointed at Jade. "With that headstrong girl, you make a good point."

Another point clarified for the good of the family. Every day brought progress. Maybe by the time Jade and Carter were grown, they'd have this parenting thing figured out.

After they put the kids to bed that night, Sophie asked Kevin if he could stay and go over some of the paperwork she'd been handling.

"If you make me some of your fancy coffee. Maybe that raspberry one?"

"Fine, but don't ask for shortbread cookies." She added water to the coffee machine.

He opened the pantry door and looked over his shoulder at her. "Are you saying you ate 'em all?"

She wasn't usually a nervous eater, but these last few weeks would give anyone the munchies. "I'm not saying anything." She added fresh coffee grounds to the machine.

They settled into the office with their mugs. She sat behind the desk, and he made himself comfortable on the sofa.

"I've filled out the forms for the mortgage insurance. The life insurance has been processed and a check should arrive for the trust this coming week." She flipped open the folder of paperwork. "We've got some decisions to make."

"Okay." He dragged the word out slowly.

"We need to make wills. I hope and pray nothing else tragic happens in Jade's and Carter's lives, but we need to be prepared." She didn't know how Kevin would feel about this discussion. A lot of people considered talk of wills and death to be morbid and refused to do it.

He took a sip of coffee. "That's probably going to be complicated. I'm sure Jackson could advise us. I have no idea how to handle trusts and things like that. You'll know a lot more about that than I do."

She was glad he didn't resist the conversation. "We'll have to consider our personal lives and the lives of the children."

"The personal part is easy. I'll make you my beneficiary. That would help you with the kids if anything happened to me."

She hadn't expected that. He'd just promised her all his earthly goods in the event of his death. Most people took ages to make such a huge decision. She'd thought about it for days and hadn't come to a firm solution, and right off the top of his head he'd landed on the best solution. "That's a good idea. I can do the same for you."

"You don't need to do that." He shifted his position

on the sofa. Perhaps he wasn't as relaxed as she'd first thought him to be.

"It's a smart choice. I don't know why I didn't think of it." She jotted down a note on the list she was making for Jackson.

"Only if you're sure. And think about it. You can let me know later what you decide."

"I'm sure." She leaned back in the chair and took a slow breath. "We also need to decide who to name as guardians."

Kevin's sober eyes met hers. "That's a huge decision."

She nodded her agreement, and they sat in silence, both searching their hearts and minds for a viable choice.

She leaned forward and propped her elbows on the desk. "What about Jackson and Allison?"

His took time to think before he answered. "They're good people. Young. He's got a solid career, and so does she. They're stable. Christian. She's sweet and they seem like they'd be great parents."

"That's what I was thinking. And I know they want kids."

Kevin set his coffee on the side table and leaned forward with his elbows on his knees. "Would they want someone else's children if they had their own?"

"We'd have to ask. And choosing them doesn't mean they'd automatically accept." She was trying to hold it together emotionally, but why did every decision have to be so important?

"True. Do you have any other suggestions? While we're talking about it, we may as well go over all the possibilities."

"I don't. Most of our friends already have a family or aren't ready to have kids yet. Honestly, the point is to choose someone who represents the same spiritual values and perspectives that Logan and Caitlyn held. That's why they chose us. They trusted us to raise the kids the way they would have."

"And we will." Sincere words from a sincere heart. That was one of the things she loved about Kevin.

Loved?

She loved Kevin?

Her breath caught in her throat, sending her into a coughing fit. Kevin raced to the kitchen and came back with a glass of water.

"Are you okay?" He stood over her at the desk and waited while she drank the water.

When she tried to speak, the words got tied up on her tongue. How did you tell your friendly fiancé that you'd just discovered you were in love with him? That you'd never stopped loving him, only you didn't know it until the exact moment you sat at a desk planning for the end of your life. A life you could no longer imagine without him in it.

The revelation could never be uttered.

Instead, she nodded and drank the rest of the water. "Sorry, I had a tickle in my throat." She put the glass on the desk. "Thank you for your help."

And for being in my life. So close that I can touch your hand, yet so far away—because of my past rejection— that I'll never be able to reach your heart.

Chapter Ten

Sophie and Kevin met with Jackson on Tuesday afternoon to discuss their wills. Making such monumental decisions was surreal to Sophie. She made business decisions and handled the finances for several local businesses on a daily basis. But the finality of deciding who would get her retirement account and other assets when she died was uncomfortable at best. The acknowledgment of her mortality, in the face of becoming a guardian, left her drained. She sat at the desk staring into space a full half hour after Jackson left the house.

"Fettuccine Alfredo?" Kevin interrupted her thoughts.

She stirred and turned to him. "What?"

"For supper?"

"Whatever you want is fine."

He scratched his forehead. "Great. Spicy chicken wings, fried onion rings and frozen chocolate pie." He turned on his heel and headed out of the office.

That pulled her from her thoughts. "Wait a minute." She followed him into the kitchen. "You win. I'm listening now. What did you really want for dinner?"

"Chicken wings, onion rings and pie." He grinned

at her. "But I know you don't like onions, so you can have fries."

"Make sure you get extra spicy sauce for Carter." She opened the refrigerator. "What about waffles, eggs and bacon?"

"Okay, you win." He pulled the waffle iron out of the drawer by the stove. "But for lunch tomorrow, I'm going to The Wing Bucket."

Sophie made a note on the grocery list that hung on the refrigerator door. "Good thing I'm ordering groceries to pick up tomorrow."

"Why?" He dug in the utensil drawer for a measuring spoon.

"We're out of antacids."

They worked together to make dinner and feed the kids. Sophie was happy that she'd learned enough to help Kevin. Happier still that it was becoming normal to be in the middle of this new family. Fatigue and grief were slowly sliding out of the forefront of every moment, even just an hour after she'd created a will necessitated by her guardianship of these little humans.

"Waffles are yummy." Jade dragged her last bite of waffle through the lake of syrup she'd asked Kevin to pour onto her plate.

"They are yummy." Sophie caught Jade's hand at the wrist and used a baby wipe on her fingers. "And sticky."

Kevin took Carter's empty plate to the sink. "Bath time for you two." He cleaned Carter's hands and took him out of the high chair.

Sophie popped the last bite of bacon into her mouth. "Mmm."

"So, you liked your dinner, too, Soapy?" Kevin grinned at her.

"Uh-huh." She put her plate in the dishwasher. "I can run the bathwater or load the dishwasher. Your choice."

"I'll do the dishes, since you helped cook."

"That's fair. Cooking is your job." She tossed him the dishcloth and headed down the hall.

Forty-five minutes later, the kids climbed onto Jade's bed and asked for a story. They were adorable in their clean pj's, snuggling into the pillows together.

Sophie snapped their picture with her phone and knelt on the floor by the bed. "What story do you want tonight? A princess or a dinosaur?"

"Princess."

"Dino."

They both shouted their answers.

Kevin sat on the end of the bed with a book upside down in his lap. "How about a princess and a dragon?" He flipped the book over to show them the princess in a long pink gown standing on the balcony of a castle turret and a smiling green dragon as tall as the castle.

"Yay." Jade clapped.

Carter watched his sister carefully, mimicked her motions. "Yay."

Nighttime stories and prayers were Sophie's new favorite time of day. The story took ten minutes, then came the prayers.

It was Sophie's turn.

"Bow your heads and close your eyes."

The children sat up in bed, clasped their hands together in front of them and waited.

Sophie captured this picture in her heart. She didn't need a camera to remember how precious the love of God that grew in their young souls was.

"Dear Lord, bless Jade and Carter, Uncle K and me. Thank You for happy stories and nighttime prayers."

Jade interrupted, "And waffles."

Kevin peeked at Sophie and smiled. She knew he was as moved as she was.

"Let everyone sleep well and have happy dreams. Amen."

"And give Mommy and Daddy happy dreams, too. Amen." Jade opened her eyes and held her arms wide. "Hugs and kisses."

Sophie wrapped them both in a hug and kissed them on the cheek. "I love you both so much."

"Wuv." Carter kissed her cheek and smiled.

Kevin leaned in for a hug, too.

"Now kiss Soapy." Jade snuggled under her blanket without taking her eyes off them.

"Carter gave me a kiss, sweetie." Sophie tucked the quilt around her shoulders after Kevin helped Carter climb off the bed.

"Not Carter. Uncle K." Jade pulled Rosie and Sissy close. "Daddy always kissed Mommy night-night. So, you kiss Soapy. Daddy said everybody needs kisses. Every day."

Sophie looked at Kevin. She was lost. Completely lost at what to say or do. Her face flamed hot.

"Daddy was right." Kevin smiled and tweaked the tip of Jade's nose.

"But—" Sophie took a step away from him when he turned.

He leaned close to her with his back to Jade. "But what?" he whispered. "I am not about to tell that little girl that what her daddy said isn't true. Are you?"

She offered him the tiniest shake of her head. He was right.

"I wanna see." Jade sat up in the bed.

"Yes, ma'am." Kevin laughed, taking Sophie by the shoulders and shifting her so Jade could see both of them.

Kevin was about to kiss her. For the first time in ten years. She wasn't ready for the beating of her heart that pounded in her ears or the hope that threatened to overwhelm her. She prayed every day for God to help her keep her feelings under control so she wouldn't do anything to hurt her growing friendship with Kevin.

Kevin kissing her wasn't the answer she expected.

He leaned forward slowly, put one finger under her chin and tilted her face toward his. As he came closer, she let her eyelids drift downward until they closed. She breathed in the earthy scent of his cologne. Perfection. His lips touched her forehead in a featherlight caress, sweeter than any she could have imagined.

The man craved competition and excitement. Adventure was in his soul. But when a little girl asked him to give his temporary fiancée a good-night kiss, he answered with the patience and tenderness of a true gentleman.

He slid his hands down her arms and captured her hands in his, linking their fingers. The comfort of his grasp settled her racing heart, and she opened her eyes. He stared into her soul.

"Like that, Jade?"

"You're silly, Uncle K. Daddy kissed Mommy on the lips." She giggled and lay back against her pillows.

Sophie took a breath and slid her hands out of his. She couldn't do that. Not even for Jade.

"You're the silly one, Jade." Sophie rearranged the quilt. "It's time for sleep."

Kevin took Carter's hand and led him out of the room. She could hear the two of them chatting as Kevin tucked the boy into his crib.

In the hallway, she turned toward the living area, then halted and took a step toward her room. She reversed direction again just as Kevin came out of Carter's room, and they collided.

"Whoa." He caught her arms to prevent her from falling.

She held a finger to his lips before she realized what she was doing. He opened his eyes wider and stood perfectly still.

"Night-night," Carter called out from his crib.

Sophie muffled a laugh and tiptoed past Carter's room while Kevin told him good-night again and closed his door.

As soon as Kevin came into the kitchen, Sophie froze in her tracks. She'd been headed to the office and had stopped to get a glass of water.

He pointed behind her. "I thought I'd take out the trash on the way to my truck."

"Oh, sure." She edged to one side to allow him room to pass. The large kitchen space seemed to shrink as he came near.

"I'm sorry about that." He pointed over his shoulder in the direction of Jade's room.

She shrugged and shook her head in a tight, quick motion. "Kids. You never know what they're gonna say." She took a long gulp of water.

"Yeah, kids." He tied up the trash bag and lifted it out of the can. "Well, I'm going to head home then." He angled his head toward the door. He sounded as nervous as she felt.

"I'll say good-night, then." As soon as she said the words she wanted them back. The heat in her cheeks betrayed her.

"Yeah. We already said that." He pulled his bottom lip between his teeth on one side. "I'll see you tomorrow, Soapy."

She wrapped her arms around her middle. "Okay." She didn't move from her spot by the sink.

At the door he paused without turning to look at her. "Did I mess up in there?"

Time stood still and she formed careful words. "No. You were sweet."

He looked at her then. "So were you."

Before she could think of a response, he left. The door shut behind him with a click.

She rubbed her fingers across her forehead.

Life was too complicated. The simple request of a little girl had twisted the relationship Sophie was trying to keep under control into a deeper, more emotional turmoil.

Kevin parked his truck on the street in front of the kids' house on Thursday morning and looked over at Chad in the passenger seat. "It's go time."

He opened the door as one of his company delivery trucks backed into the driveway and blew the horn.

Chad slammed the passenger door shut. "I hope you know what you're doing. Sophie doesn't seem to be the kind of woman who likes a lot of surprises."

"This is for the kids. They'll love it, so she'll love it, too."

Chad joined him at the back of the company truck. "Don't say you weren't warned."

"What's the harm in a few little presents?"

Sophie walked onto the porch carrying Carter and holding Jade's hand. "Hi." The kids waved at him. "What's going on out here?"

Kevin met her on the front walk and picked Jade up. "I've got some surprises." He couldn't hide his smile when the men opened the back doors of the delivery truck to reveal a stack of boxes containing a swing set, a large climbing toy in the shape of a pirate ship and all the accessories he could imagine they might need to transform the backyard.

"Boxes?" Jade pointed into the truck. "I like boxes." She wiggled in an effort to get down.

"Not just boxes, Jade. A swing set and a pirate ship. And a lot of other stuff to make it all fun."

She scrunched her face and patted his cheek. "Like a playground?"

He gave her an exaggerated nod. "Exactly like a playground."

Sophie hadn't said a word. Probably because it was such a great surprise. "What do you think, Soapy?"

"I think it's a surprise." Her blank expression could mean anything. Displeasure, uncertainty. A myriad of emotions could be credited to her reaction.

Kevin waved for his crew to unload the boxes. The first one out of the truck was the pirate ship. They set it on the grass by the driveway.

"Carter, you can climb on this and be the captain." He pointed out the children playing in the picture on the label. "We'll have so much fun."

"I can be a pirate, too." Jade put her hand on the little girl in the picture. "And Rosie and Sissy can play, too."

Still silence from Sophie. Kevin began to wonder if Chad had been right. He darted a glance at Chad and caught the remains of a smirk.

The men set the swing set box on the ground.

Chad brushed his palms off on his khaki uniform pants and went to stand by Sophie. "He bought the latest and greatest that we carry in the store. I think he's determined to spoil these kids."

"It looks like it." Sophie smiled at Chad.

Not to be deterred, Kevin took Jade to see the swing set picture. "You loved the park, so I wanted to put a little park in the backyard for you and Carter. See that swing? That's for big girls like you." He showed Carter a smaller box that contained a swing designed for toddlers. "And that one's for you. It's just the right size, so you can go high and not fall."

Chad and his men continued to unload the back of the truck. Kevin showed the kids each box and hoped Sophie would show some enthusiasm for his gifts.

Since the expo, things had been good between them. They'd had mostly pleasant days. The kids were adjusting to them being there all the time.

Sophie had made the house a home for herself, too. At first, she hadn't wanted to change things from the way Caitlyn had them, and then they'd agreed it was necessary. She'd put up some of her pictures in the office and her bedroom. He'd noticed several things in the kitchen that she'd added. True, it was mostly things to do with her beloved coffee machine.

He'd taken over the guest room as his own. So far, she'd refused any offer he made to stay overnight and let her have a break by staying at her mom's, but he could tell she was warming up to the idea.

She didn't seem to be warming up to the swing set, though.

"Chad, I'm going to help Sophie get the kids inside. I'll be out back to help in a few minutes." He bounced Jade on his hip as he walked up the sidewalk. She wrapped her arms around his neck and held on tight, giggling until he set her on the rug inside the front door. "Let's see if we can open the blinds so you and Carter can watch us work."

He moved Carter's play yard and toys close to the window that overlooked the backyard. Both kids seemed fascinated by the men moving the boxes—until they weren't. He and Sophie barely had them settled in their new spot before they started playing with their toys and jabbering to each other in what he'd come to think of as sibling-speak.

Sophie stood by the play yard looking out the window as the boxes were stacked near the back porch.

"Well, what do you think? You haven't said anything except that it's a surprise." He tried not to be hurt, but this was a big thing for him. It was his first grand gesture as a parent.

She didn't answer as she pursed her lips and twisted them to one side, still not looking at him.

"Uh-oh. I know that look."

"It's a lot of nice stuff. I think they'll really like it."

"But? I can hear a *but* in there." He couldn't think what her objection might be.

She glanced at him and turned back to the window. "I thought we'd agreed to do things together—make decisions together and talk to one another. That whole *united front* concept. By talking." He could hear the disappointment in her voice, and he felt like an idiot.

He rapped his knuckles on the window and signaled for Chad and the guys to stop working. "I messed up. I can take it all back. Right now. The crew can load it back into the truck." He glanced over at the kids. "They only saw the pictures, not the actual stuff. We can close the blinds, and if they ask about it later, I'll tell them I had to go back to work and we can't build it today. They'll forget. They're little." He wasn't sure he'd ever babbled before, but he was doing it now.

She let out a little burst of laughter and covered her mouth to stop it.

"Please, tell me how to fix this. I'm fresh out of ideas." He was like a fish out of water. No matter how much effort he put into things, he made no progress.

"I'd say you have plenty of ideas." She pointed at the boxes outside the window. "I do need to correct one tiny point." She held up one hand with her thumb and index finger close together. "One tiny, little point. They won't forget. They don't forget. I think forgetfulness is a sign of aging, because those two don't forget anything. It's like the younger you are, the more you can remember for longer. One day I promised them they could watch a video the next afternoon. The entire next day Jade asked me every fifteen minutes if it was time yet."

"Another lesson in parenting. Got it. So, what should I do?"

"We should decide where to put all this stuff." She looked back at him with an open expression. "And tonight, after the kids are in bed, we need to figure out what part of the budget it's coming out of."

He knocked on the window again and gave Chad the go-ahead to get back to work.

Kevin checked on the kids and came to stand behind her at the window as she watched his crew. "I'll show you where I was thinking of putting everything, and you can tell me what your ideas are." He leaned one arm against the window seal and spoke close to her ear. "But this is my gift to the kids—and to you. My first parental *ta-da*. It'll be fun for them. I hope it will be a bright spot in your days with them. They loved the park. That's when I got the idea."

Sophie reached up one hand and pulled her ponytail over her shoulder. The tropical scent of her shampoo wafted in front of his face. She twisted to look at him. "Thank you. It's a very sweet gift."

Her smile was like a gift to him. Being close to her and sharing a moment of joy for their kids was worth more than anything he could ever buy. He could get used to this part of family life.

"It's my pleasure."

Chad's piercing whistle caught their attention. He stood in the middle of the backyard and shrugged with his hands out, palms up.

Kevin lowered his arm and stepped back from Sophie at the same time she moved toward the play yard.

"I think the assembly crew wants us to hurry up. They work hard and fast, but they aren't their happiest if I make them late for lunch."

Together they decided where to put the various pieces. By the end of the workday, everything Kevin had purchased was assembled and in its place.

"Thanks, guys. You did a great job." He waved as the men drove away from the house.

Sophie called to him from the front door. "I don't think I can make them wait another minute. If you want to see them on the swings for the first time, you better be quick."

They conquered the pirate ship, played on the slide and squealed with delight when he and Sophie pushed them in the swings. The sun was almost gone when they dragged the kids inside with the promise of more play the next day if the weather permitted. Exhaustion kept them from putting up much of an argument.

That evening, Kevin turned on Carter's night-light and closed the bedroom door. The child had fallen asleep as soon as his head hit the pillow. Kevin heard soft snores coming from Jade's room when he passed.

He stopped in his room and grabbed a light jacket from the closet. The air had chilled since they'd come in from the backyard. He shrugged his arms into the sleeves as he walked down the hall.

Sophie sat on the sofa with her feet on the ottoman. He wasn't sure she was awake until she moved her arm onto a throw pillow.

"I'm going to head home." He fastened the zipper and pulled the tab up to his chest.

"They love it. All of it." Her voice was soft with fatigue.

"Yeah. They do, don't they?" He had never given a gift that brought him more joy in such a short time. He was so glad she'd agreed to let them keep everything. He'd consult her in the future, but he'd cherish the memory of surprising the kids today.

"Good job, Uncle K."

"Get some rest. I'll lock the door on my way out."

She lifted one hand in a silent goodbye. He knew she'd be asleep before he left the driveway.

Today had been hard work. The assembly crew from the store had used their expertise to make the physical labor happen in a just a few hours.

The forging of a family of four people who never imagined they'd be a family was more delicate work. A type of spiritual heart surgery bound them together in love. Days like today, when they experienced it together, made the effort worthwhile.

"I'm glad you came, Mom. It's good for the kids to spend time with you."

Sophie had worked that morning while Kevin tended to the children. Her mother had arrived after lunch. Kevin offered to clean up the kitchen while everyone else played in the yard.

"It's my Saturday off." Diane helped Carter into his toddler swing. "Besides, I love being here."

"You know, the kids never had any grandparents before. I'm glad they'll have that in you."

"Me, too." Diane pushed the swing for Carter, and he giggled. "Are you sure they're warm enough?"

"Coats, hats and mittens are enough." Sophie smiled at her mom while she pushed Jade in the swing.

The kids were having fun, but a late January cold front was making its way across Texas. They wouldn't be outside for long today.

"Sophie, you're doing a wonderful job with the kids. You and Kevin both are."

"Thanks, Mom. You're sweet to say so. We're doing our best."

Diane focused her gaze on Carter while they talked. "Can I tell you something?"

"Sure." Sophie pulled Jade's hat back over her ears and gave her another push.

"I'm happy you're engaged."

"I'm happy, too." Even if she wouldn't confide in her mother about her love for Kevin, it was nice to admit she was glad they were engaged. She and Kevin had saved the children from leaving their home and starting a new life with strangers. That was worth a temporary arrangement. She refused to think about how she'd feel when it ended.

"At first, I didn't know what to think. It was out of character for you to do something so important, so quickly. You've been so cautious about everything in your life, since—" she cleared her throat "—since your father's accident."

Diane pointed at the kids. "I was afraid you were both reacting to your situation and you might be headed for more heartache. Now that you're in love, I don't have to worry anymore." She looked straight at Sophie with a motherly look that defied resistance. "You are in love, aren't you?"

Sophie pulled her lips between her teeth and swallowed. Heat filled her face in spite of the cooler weather. Her voice came out in a whisper. "I am."

"He's a good man, Sophie."

She nodded. "I know." She hated that she couldn't tell her mother that Kevin didn't return her love. The fact that he was a good man meant she could never tell him.

He'd honor his word to be with her as a friend for the sake of the children. It wouldn't be fair, after she'd hurt him so deeply when they were young, to tell him that she loved him. It could ruin their newly restored friendship.

She'd ruined their relationship once. She wouldn't risk doing it again.

If she kept talking with her mother, she feared she'd pour out her heart, and everything she and Kevin had worked to build for the kids could be in jeopardy. She'd said too much.

"Last time, Jade." Sophie pushed her new daughter. "It's getting too chilly, so we need to go inside."

Diane pushed Carter forward. "This is the last push for you, too. Your nose is pink, little guy. Like Soapy's face."

Her mother's sneaky grin made the heat flare hotter in Sophie's cheeks.

They all rushed inside and closed the door to block out the cooling temperatures.

"Brrr. Off with your coat." Diane helped Carter out of his mittens and hat.

"I'm not cold." Jade's lips started to quiver when she protested being back indoors.

"Well, I'm very cold, and I would be lonely in here without you." Sophie slipped Jade's hat off and smoothed the static out of her flyway hair.

A shiver ran over the little girl. "Well, if *you* need me." She put her hand in Sophie's. "Let's sit by the fireplace." She wagged a bossy finger. "But not too close. It's dang'ous."

Sophie smiled and sat on the rug with Jade. "It smells delicious in here, Kevin."

The oven timer beeped, and Kevin turned it off. "I made a treat for everyone who played nice in the backyard."

"Brownies!" Jade jumped to her feet.

Sophie caught her before she dashed into the kitchen. "Wait just a minute. Are you supposed to be in the kitchen when Uncle K is cooking?"

Jade frowned and crossed her arms. "I want a brownie."

"Be a good girl, and you'll get one, but the oven is dangerous, just like the fireplace. Never, ever run in the kitchen." Sophie tugged Jade into her lap and hugged her close. "Promise?"

"I promise." Jade huffed out a sigh and hugged Sophie back. She wound her little fingers into Sophie's hair and used her softest pleading tone. "Now can I have a brownie?"

Sophie laughed and tickled her tummy. "After they cool."

A few minutes later Kevin cut the brownies and called everyone to the kitchen island. "Who wants ice cream on their brownie?"

She raised her eyebrows. "Really?"

He shrugged. "A treat is supposed to be special."

Diane opened the freezer and pulled out the ice cream. "Indulge the man, Sophie. After all, isn't he in charge of the kitchen?"

Kevin leaned on the counter and caught Sophie's gaze. "You know, your mother is a smart lady. You should listen to her." He winked at her and Sophie wished with all her might that she could control the heat flooding into her face again.

It became more and more apparent to her that her

heart was going to make its presence known. She had a lot to think and pray about. Maybe ice cream and brownies were just the thing to distract her for the moment.

She refused to think about how short-lived that moment would be.

Chapter Eleven

❦

"I'm gonna get you." Kevin crawled across the rug after Carter. He'd do almost anything to hear the bubbly belly laugh that only babies could do.

Carter squealed and scooted as fast as his chubby arms and legs would take him. He lost his balance and rolled over to his side. Kevin tickled him and flipped him back over so he could scamper away again. Sunday evenings were fast becoming Kevin's favorite part of the week.

"Boys are noisy." Jade sat on the sofa with Rosie and Sissy.

"So are girls." Kevin grabbed her sock-covered feet and tickled her toes.

Jade wiggled and twisted until she freed her feet, then jumped on Kevin's back as he crawled away.

Sophie opened the office door and came into the room. Kevin grabbed the two kids and sat with them on the rug as if they'd been still and quiet for the last half hour.

"Hi, Soapy." He grinned at her over the top of the children's heads. "Wanna play?"

She took several slow steps toward them. "I don't know. What's the name of this quiet game where everyone sits on the rug without talking?" Her eyes were wide as she teased the kids. "Are you sure you want to play like that?" She dropped onto the rug with them. "Or would you rather play ponies?"

Kevin burst out laughing at Sophie's attempt to whinny.

"Horsey!" Jade climbed onto Kevin's back again and pushed his shoulders to get him to crawl around the room. She grabbed the collar of his shirt and pulled as if she held the reins of a real horse, choking and delighting him at the same time.

"Come here, you." Sophie pulled Carter onto her back and followed Kevin around the rug.

They played well past the kids' bedtime and had to rush through the process of getting them into their pj's.

"One short story and prayers." Sophie tucked Jade into her bed and settled into her spot on the floor beside her.

Kevin read the story, and Sophie said the prayers. Carter and Jade echoed her amen.

He picked Carter up and offered a hand to help Sophie to stand. She accepted and released him, but not as quickly as she had in the past.

What did her lingering touch mean? Did he even want to find out?

Jade turned onto her side and snuggled into the pillow. "Don't forget the kisses."

Sophie kissed her temple, and Kevin kissed her hand like the prince in the story he'd read. "Good night, Jade."

"Good night, Uncle K." Her eyes drooped with fatigue. "Kiss Soapy, too."

"Yes, ma'am." He reached for Sophie's hand again, and she slipped it into his. With a slight squeeze of her fingers, he leaned over and kissed Sophie's hair. Since he'd kissed her forehead before, he'd fought to hide feelings he needed to suppress. He didn't want either of them to be uncomfortable, but they'd agreed it was important for the kids to see affection in their family.

For years he'd protected his heart from *any* woman—especially Sophie.

Thanks to Jade, the good-night kisses had become a part of their nightly rituals. He savored the moments. These children had softened his scarred heart.

No amount of talking to himself had convinced Kevin that he only wanted to kiss Sophie for the kids' sake. No. He wanted to take her in his arms and share his true heart with her. To give her a kiss full of promise and dedication. A kiss of hope.

Did he dare to hope? What if he opened up to Sophie and she rejected him again? Being wounded by her now could cause the scars to heal over so tightly that he might never allow himself to be vulnerable again.

Hope or rejection. Both thoughts scared him.

Not like the adrenaline rush of an adventure—more like a life-or-death choice he could regret forever.

Carter nodded against his shoulder and murmured in an effort to fight off slumber.

"It's your turn, little man." He tucked Carter into the crib and turned on the night-light. He stood watching him fall sleep and didn't hear Sophie join him.

She slipped her hand over his on the side of the crib and whispered, "He's beyond precious."

"He is." Kevin turned his hand over and captured hers. "We're blessed to have them in our lives."

"We are. I know they will always miss their parents, but I'm so grateful that God allowed us to be with them."

"So am I."

Kevin kept her hand in his and walked with her out of the room and down the hall. In the living room, he turned to face her. Somehow her other hand went into his.

This touch wasn't like when he'd held her hand in court as they'd clung to each other as friends drowning in grief and afraid of losing the kids. This touch was the slow and natural beginning of two people coming together.

They stood so close he could almost see his reflection in her gaze.

Neither of them said a word as they stared into each other's eyes, searching, lost in the newness of a deepening friendship. A friendship that had grown out of necessity and flourished like no other relationship he'd ever known.

The unexpected truth made his heartbeat quicken. He'd loved her before. Truly loved her. But this experience was even more than the feelings and emotions that colored his memories. The richness and gratification of counting on another person, working side by side with them, nurturing little humans as they grew—all these things made the value of this new relationship more complex than when they'd dated and fallen in love all those years ago.

The anticipation they'd thrived on when they'd talked about spending their lives together in their youth had been ignorant of the challenges they'd faced in the last few weeks. And those challenges had proved all over again what a beautiful person Sophie was, inside and out.

"Sophie, I—" He paused to look for any sign that she wouldn't be open to his heart or the words he longed to say. The only thing he found in her eyes was hope. "May I kiss you?"

One corner of her mouth lifted in a half smile. "If I can kiss you back."

"Well, fair is fair." He slid his hands up her arms and cradled her cheeks in his palms.

She leaned closer, and he lowered his mouth to hers in gentle reverence. He took nothing from her, only gave the tenderness of his heart.

He raised his head, hopeful that she didn't regret permitting his embrace.

She lifted her hands to hold his forearms and pressed her lips to his. The sweetness of her very soul touched his heart.

As she backed away, her soft smile eased his trepidation that she'd regret kissing him.

When she gazed up at him and didn't speak, he finally said, "Wow."

She nodded. "Wow."

The stillness of the moment held them captive.

He couldn't stand it any longer. "Should we talk about this?"

"Okay." She uttered the word in a measured tone.

"On the sofa?"

"On opposite ends."

Kevin bit his bottom lip. Distance could signal a warning to proceed with caution.

She sat on one end of the sectional and pulled a pillow into her lap. Her arms went around it as if it were a life preserver in a stormy sea. "Do you think we should be doing that?" She pointed to the spot where they'd kissed.

"Well, to be honest, I didn't plan it, but it was nice."

Her cheeks went the prettiest shade of pink, and she lowered her eyes to the pillow she held. "Very nice."

"Like an adventure nice." He wanted to lighten the mood. If she got too serious, she'd overthink it, and they'd have a more awkward relationship than ever.

"I warned you not to try to get me to be adventurous." Her eyes darkened with concern.

"Not a dangerous adventure, Sophie. A thrilling one. The kind where your heart races and you want to experience it all over again." He couldn't stay on the opposite end of the sofa. He moved next to her. "A sweet memory to look back on and cherish. No pain involved."

"Promise?"

"Not to hurt you?"

"Yes."

"Oh, Sophie, I can promise that I'll never hurt you on purpose. I can promise that I'll do my best to be cautious, but I can't promise there will never be pain in our relationship—no matter what kind of relationship it is. We've already disagreed about things since we got the kids, but we've worked everything out. Haven't we? It's been worth the effort so far."

"We have, haven't we? But the kids are the reason."

"We're good friends." He needed to know what she was thinking. "What scares you the most?"

"If you'd asked me yesterday, I'd have said I'm afraid of the judge finding out we aren't really engaged like he thinks we are."

"And tonight?"

She lifted her shoulders in a slight shrug. "I'm afraid we might be headed toward something real, and the children could be hurt if we explore that possibility and it doesn't work. We've failed before."

His gut clenched. Within moments of taking the leap to show her he might be willing to open his heart, she had backed away in fear.

Everything inside of him wanted to jump up and pace the room, to run his fingers through his hair and spout off a list of all the reasons fear could keep her from happiness—and maybe even love. But Sophie didn't decide things like he did. She made lists and studied different scenarios in her mind.

"That's a fair statement." He wouldn't push her. Pressure made her bolt. She'd done it before, and this time there was too much at stake. The sleeping kids down the hall needed their guardians to be stable and true. "We'll honor our commitment to each other and the kids. And we'll do what we promised in the beginning—stay focused on permanent guardianship. That's the most important thing."

"That's probably for the best."

He pointed over his shoulder at the front door, not looking away from her. "I'm going to go then. It's been quite a Sunday. The best I've had in a long time."

"It was nice." Timidity filled her tone.

He wanted to believe they could conquer their past and create a new future, but his faith wasn't strong enough to conquer her fear.

He waved and left her.

Sophie sensed a bit of awkwardness for a few minutes after Kevin arrived on Monday, but they settled in to take care of the kids. That night when Jade asked him to kiss Sophie, he'd kissed her cheek.

Sunday's brief encounter faded to a memory.

Sophie missed Kevin's help on Tuesday morning. He'd gone to Dallas to try out some new sporting equipment to decide if he wanted to stock it in his store.

She'd resisted the urge to ask if he'd be in danger. In her case, fear of the known might be greater than fear of the unknown. If she didn't know he was scaling a rock wall or zip-lining with new equipment he'd never used, she'd probably worry less.

Probably.

By the time he came home that evening, she had conquered her concerns and was getting the kids ready for bed.

Jade launched into a speech as soon as he came into her room. "Uncle K, we didn't play outside today. Soapy said it was too cold. Did you go outside today?"

"I did." His smile included Sophie and the kids.

"Did you get cold?"

"A little bit. Soapy was right to make you stay inside." He looked at Sophie, and she nodded her approval of his support.

"Time for prayers." Sophie shifted Carter on the bed beside his sister, but he raised his arms for Kevin to pick him up.

Kevin's expression in response to Carter's natural affection for him was precious. "Come here, big guy. Did you miss me? Did you?" He snuggled the child against his shoulder and sat on the end of the bed. "Whose turn is it to pray?"

"Mine." Jade folded her hands and stared at all of them until they closed their eyes. Only then did she start her prayers. "Dear Jesus, thank You for our new slide and swings. And for Soapy and Uncle K. Thank You for french fries and ketchup. Amen."

"Oh, my. I'm excited that I made it into your fries and ketchup prayer." Sophie straightened the quilt and kissed the child's cheek. "I love you, Jade."

"I love you, Soapy, and Uncle K, and Carter." She twisted onto her side and put her hands together under one cheek. "We're a happy family."

Tears stung Sophie's eyes. "We sure are." She brushed Jade's hair away from her face and kissed her again.

"You're a sweet girl, Jade." Kevin's raspy voice wavered when he leaned down to kiss her good night. "Sleep well."

"Kiss Soapy." Jade's eyes were closing as she repeated her nightly command.

Kevin kissed her on the cheek again and smiled at her. Between the three of them, her family had her at the point of tears tonight. Happy tears of gratitude that they'd forged the family they all needed.

She'd been right to resist trying to change her relationship with Kevin. These moments were too precious to risk.

After they put Carter down for the night, Sophie made decaf coffee for them, and they sat at the kitchen island together. "How was your trip to Dallas?"

"Good. We're going to carry the new line of climbing equipment. It's a new company, but they make a quality product with safety as their top priority. Plus, their pricing is competitive. It was worth the trip."

"I'm glad."

He must have noticed the hesitation in her voice. "I didn't tell you what kind of equipment I'd be testing because I didn't think you'd want to know."

"I didn't." She wrapped her hands around her warm mug. "And then I did." She shrugged. "Let's just say I'm adjusting."

"Anytime you want to know, please ask. I won't go into details unless you want me to."

"Thanks." She hated that part of her—a huge part— still worried about his safety. She didn't know if she'd ever get over the fear that drove her worry.

"How about your day? Were you stuck inside the whole time?"

"Pretty much, but the kids were good. I actually made it through most of my work while they napped and played. I'm getting better at multitasking. The January accounts are almost in the books. It's a tough month for me, but I made it."

She held up her mug. "Only by the grace of God and caffeine. That's why I switched to decaf for tonight. I intend to sleep like a baby."

"It's better for me, too." He took another sip from his mug.

"I even finished your accounting. Your office manager is excellent. Everything was in great shape, and I was able to make some suggestions for ways to improve your bottom line. I'll send you a copy tonight when I email everything to her."

"I like the sound of that."

"Oh. While you were out of town today, Jackson called."

He twisted on the stool to face her. "Is everything okay? You sound concerned. You could have called me."

"He said he tried to call you and didn't get an answer. He doesn't think there's anything to worry about, but Judge Carlisle is ill. He's postponing our court date for next Tuesday. Jackson said his clerk will let us know the new time."

His face relaxed. "Okay. As long as there's not a problem with finalizing the guardianship."

"He didn't think so. He actually said everything is a formality at this point. He's seen all the reports that were sent to the judge. Nothing showed up that would prevent the judge from finalizing us as permanent guardians for the kids."

Kevin set his cup on the counter. "That's the best news of all."

"It is. I was so worried, what with the judge's eccentricities and all. I asked Jackson, and he said once the paperwork is filed we can set our minds at ease because then the kids will be ours." She hoped Jackson was right.

"Thank the Lord. It's what we all wanted. Logan, Caitlyn, you, me—all of us." His happiness was contagious.

"This is the first time we've talked about the guardianship that I've felt joy instead of wanting to cry."

He smiled at her. "'Weeping may endure for the night, but joy comes in the morning.'"

"I'll be glad to see the dawn of the day when all the legal matters are behind us."

"It's happening. We just need to accept it." He let out a big sigh.

"I'm trying." She refilled her coffee cup. "But tonight, I have a few more files to finish."

He put his cup in the dishwasher and turned it on. "I better get going."

"Thanks for coming tonight. I know you must be tired." She followed him to the door.

"I wouldn't have missed it. This family has become

my world." His eyes were full of thoughts she couldn't decipher. "I'll see you in the morning."

He slipped out the door before she could ask.

Thank You, Lord, for creating a family—unconventional as it is—out of the darkness we've all come through.

She'd long ago given up hope of having the kind of life she was living today. Three people counted on her— three people she grew to love more every day.

Old dreams had died, and new ones took their place. Hope stirred her soul. Hope she didn't know she'd lost so completely until it opened her up again, like a budding flower in spring, and began to fill her life with joy.

The joy was short-lived. Jackson called late the next morning to tell them the judge had moved the case out two weeks and warned them to be prepared to make their application for adoption when they came.

He dropped the drastic warning with all the finesse of a seasoned attorney. "According to his clerk, Judge Carlisle has decided that you've been engaged long enough. He expects you to marry, then, instead of guardianship, he'll approve you and Kevin for adoption."

"Long enough?" She couldn't believe what she was hearing. It had only been a matter of weeks.

"Remember how Kevin told the judge it was like you'd been engaged for a year? Apparently, he thinks that's long enough."

She disconnected the call and leaned against the kitchen island, forgetting to breathe. This couldn't be happening. She had to tell Kevin as soon as possible. But first, she had to catch her breath.

Kevin brought a lunch of sub sandwiches and kids' meals immediately after she called and told him the news.

"What is this man trying to do?" Frustration punctuated every syllable. He pulled the food out of the bags while he talked, and she poured milk into the kids' cups. "Wield his power? I don't know? From the way Jackson talked, Judge Carlisle was trying to clear up as many cases as he can as quickly as possible. He hinted that the judge might be facing a medical retirement and wanted to clear his docket before making the announcement."

"So, we go from waiting for him to retire in two years, so we can have control of our lives back, to him deciding our fate on his way out of office?"

"I guess." She shrugged and lifted Carter into his high chair. "Here you go, Carter. Uncle K got you apple slices. Yummy."

She needed to keep calm in front of the kids, but she wanted to pace the porch like Kevin to see if it would alleviate a fragment of her anxiety.

Carter grabbed an apple slice in one chubby fist and his milk cup in the other. "P'ay."

Jade climbed onto her stool. "My turn." She launched into the blessing without warning and was finished before Sophie could close her eyes.

"Are you hungry, Jade?" Kevin tousled her blond hair and slid her plate in front of her.

The kids proved a pleasant if temporary distraction.

"We get to go outside after lunch. Soapy said it's not too cold."

Kevin turned to Sophie. "I'm guessing this is another case of children not forgetting anything you tell them."

"Yes. Every spoken word to a child is received as a promise."

They ate and then took the kids into the backyard.

She and Kevin sat on the back porch in Adirondack chairs and watched the kids play inside the pirate ship.

Sophie expressed her angst to Kevin. "I can't believe we went from permanent guardianship to adoption—on the condition we marry first—in one day."

"I called Jackson on my way here. He seemed as concerned as he was that first day in court. He still thinks it's the only way to guarantee that the kids will be with us."

"But we talked about this. If it goes wrong between us, we can ruin everything."

"At this point, I don't know what else we can do."

"It's a huge step. I mean, would you be willing to do that? I think we need to have Jackson tell Judge Carlisle we've decided on a long engagement. A lot of people are engaged for more than a year. We can tell him we're getting everything in order for the kids. I'm still knee-deep in paperwork for Logan and Caitlyn's finances."

Sophie decided her life had become a giant roller coaster she hadn't bought a ticket for. Her emotions went from high to low and back so fast she didn't know if she'd ever regain her equilibrium.

Kevin didn't say anything for a long moment. "Hmm. And try to get him to sign off on permanent guardianship now?"

"Yes."

"That might work. If he gets better and is on the bench for two more years, but we have the guardianship finalized, we'll be fine. If he turns out to be so sick he has to retire, we'll still avoid having to marry just because he thinks we should."

And there it was. The fact that Kevin didn't want to marry her.

She took in a slow, calming breath to keep him from noticing her pain at his words. She didn't think he even realized what he'd said.

Well, he hadn't come right out and said it, but in her heart she was convinced that's what he meant.

She plastered a smile on her face and looked him in the eye. "You're right. That's what we should do."

He nodded in agreement just as Jade let out an ear-piercing scream.

They both flew off the porch and ran to where she lay beneath the still-moving swing.

Jade sucked in another breath and cried again. "Oww!"

"Where does it hurt, baby?" Sophie knelt at her side while Kevin ran his hands lightly over her head, then one arm and the other.

"My foot." Jade sobbed and gasped for breath at the same time.

Sophie felt helpless. "How could we look away? She wasn't supposed to be on the swing. They were in the pirate ship." She knew it wasn't fair to fling the words at Kevin, but she was terrified at the thought of Jade being seriously injured. They hadn't seen her fall, so they didn't know what injuries she might possibly have.

Kevin carefully checked Jade's legs. When he got to her right ankle, she screamed again.

He spoke calmly to her. "I'm so sorry, Jade. Uncle K will be gentle. Right now, I have to see how bad you're hurt."

He cut his eyes to Sophie. "I need you to call your mother. Have her meet us at the emergency room. She can take Carter, so you and I can stay with Jade."

Tears streamed down Sophie's face. She hadn't realized she was crying until that moment. "Okay." She picked Carter up from the pirate ship, where he'd never stopped playing, and dashed inside. She grabbed the ever-ready diaper bag and car keys.

By the time she had Carter buckled into his seat, Kevin had carried Jade to the SUV and put her in her seat. He'd grabbed a small ice pack on his way through the house and tucked it into her sock. He'd even brought Rosie and Sissy along to comfort her. He was pretty amazing for a new dad.

Sophie had the vehicle in Reverse before he closed his door.

Diane met them at the hospital and took charge of Carter while Kevin carried Jade inside.

The hour they spent in the waiting room before Jade was called into an examining room passed at a torturous pace. Sophie wanted to bang on the doors and insist that they see her crying child. Why were they left sitting here in the far corner of the room for so long?

One at a time, the other patients went through the swinging doors until they were alone in the quiet room. Only the sirens of an approaching ambulance reminded her that worse cases were handled in the ER every day.

The last time she'd been here, Jade and Carter's parents had passed. The fear and dread of that night threatened to overwhelm her. Fast behind that wave of emotion came the memory of the night her father died. She'd waited for the news in this same room.

It was too much. She clamped her eyes shut in an unsuccessful effort to blot out the memories and the sorrow that came with them. A tide of fear swept over her.

Why had she agreed to let Kevin put up the swing set? They should have waited until the kids were older.

What kind of guardian sat on the porch and looked away while a child fell? This accident had been preventable.

She jerked out of her chair and paced the tile floor between the rows of plastic chairs. She rubbed her fingers against the throbbing in her temples. "What can be taking so long?" She dropped back onto the chair beside Kevin.

"She's going to be fine, Sophie." He held Jade in his lap. She'd cried herself to sleep in his arms a few minutes earlier. He reached for Sophie's hand, but she ignored him and stood to pace again.

"Look at us." Kevin chuckled under his breath. "You're going to wear out the tile, but I'm still. When did we switch roles?"

"When you brought your adventurous ways home in a delivery van." She stopped still and clapped her hand over her mouth when she heard the words. "I'm sorry, Kevin." She sat next to him again. "That wasn't fair. I'm just upset."

He withdrew. Not physically. But every other part of him backed away from her at warp speed. "I'm upset, too, but you need to think about something. She's not your dad, and she's not seriously injured."

"I know that, but it didn't have to happen. Just like Dad didn't have to buy a motorcycle, and you didn't have to jump off a platform for a thrill and ride a silly harness down a tiny cable." She caught her breath. She'd done it now. In a moment of near panic, she'd lashed out in fear and hurt the man she cared most about in the world. A man she'd committed to share her life with, for the sake of the kids. "I'm sorry. I didn't mean it."

He raised his brows. "That came from somewhere inside of you. A place I thought had healed."

In the space of two minutes, she'd destroyed the glimmer of hope she'd begun to nurture for building something greater with Kevin. She watched it die in his eyes.

"I'm so sorry. Please forgive me." She pulled on the sleeve of his jacket.

A nurse pushed open the door that divided the ER from the waiting room. She referenced a clipboard. "Jade West."

"That's us." Sophie snatched up her purse and followed Kevin as he carried their sleeping child.

Ten minutes later, they waited again. Jade was awake and very unhappy. She'd resisted the nurse and her duties with great fervor. The nurse had assured them the doctor would look at the chart and be with them as soon as possible.

"Jade, you're a brave pirate, right?" Kevin leaned his elbows on the white paper that covered the medical table and talked to her.

Jade sniffed. "Yes."

"So, a pirate waiting to see the doctor would do what?"

She stuck out her bottom lip. "Pirates don't go to the doctor."

"Really? Not even when they fall off the crow's nest while they're on the lookout for gold?" His pirate voice made Jade and Sophie smile.

"Right you are, mate." Jade giggled and mimicked his cartoonish accent. "I didn't see no gold, but I think I saw an island."

"Was there a mermaid on the shore?" Kevin kept up his game with Jade until the nurse came into the room to take Jade for an X-ray.

The nurse held up her hand when Kevin picked Jade up and Sophie followed them to the door. "Just one parent. It only takes a few minutes, and she'll come right back to this room."

They were parents now. They were responsible for this little girl. Together. They didn't have time to fight about how she got hurt—or anything else.

Kevin looked at Sophie for the first time since they'd disagreed in the waiting room. "Do you want to take her?"

"I want K." Jade wrapped her arms tightly around his neck.

"You take her." Sophie kissed Jade's temple. "Maybe there's gold in the X-ray room." She forced a smile and watched them walk down the hall and into another room.

They weren't gone long, but it was more than enough time for Sophie to replay every thoughtless word over and over again in her mind.

An hour later, Jade rode to the exit of the ER in a wheelchair. Unlike adults who protested at such a spectacle, she thought it was awesome and rode with Rosie and Sissy in her lap. Each doll wore a pink bandage on their right ankle to match Jade's.

"Rosie and Sissy need some ice c'eam. The doctor said it helps when you get hurt bad." Jade focused on the treat instead of her sprained ankle.

Kevin agreed instantly. "We'll stop by Scoopdily-icious on the way home then. We've got to get you and your babies well."

Sophie thanked the nurse who pushed Jade's chair. "I'm so sorry we overreacted."

The nurse smiled. "It's fine. Most new parents struggle with the first few issues that come up. We'd rather you erred on the side of caution. Little ones are tough, but sometimes they get into mischief and need our help. You can be looking right at them when it happens, too. Always remember that accidents happen. It's not your fault she's a curious three-year-old."

She knew the nurse was telling the truth, but she still blamed herself for not paying attention.

Kevin lifted Jade into the car and climbed into the back seat with her. Sophie watched him in the rearview mirror as she drove to Scoopdilyicious. He kept up a conversation with Jade the entire trip, and even though he included her a couple of times, the distance between them was frozen solid.

She'd wounded him, but he knew she was terrified of risks.

It was unfair to be angry. She fought against it.

Sophie had hoped she was beginning to heal. Seeing Jade hurt because Sophie hadn't paid attention brought back the torrent of fear.

By the time they got home, Sophie had gone from worry, to remorseful, and was headed toward panic at breakneck speed.

Diane opened the door when the three of them walked up the sidewalk. "How's my girl?" She admired the bandage.

"It's better now. We got ice c'eam."

"That always helps." Diane took the Scoopdilyicious take-out bag from Sophie. "I'm guessing this is a treat for Carter."

"It is." Sophie put a pillow under Jade's foot after Kevin positioned her in the corner of the sectional. "How about a princess movie?"

"My favorite one? With the butterflies?" Jade snuggled into the corner and pulled her dolls close.

"Sure." Sophie got her set up and asked her mom to watch both kids for a few minutes.

"Kevin, can we talk for a minute?"

He checked his watch before he answered. "I need to run back to the store for an hour or so. Can we do it later?"

Without waiting for an answer, he told the kids goodbye and headed out the front door.

She caught him in the driveway. "Please, Kevin. Just a minute."

He got into the driver's seat of his truck, started the motor and lowered the window. "You don't have to say anything, Sophie."

"I do. I was upset. I didn't mean it. It's not your fault Jade got hurt."

"It's not your fault, either." He closed the door and propped his elbow in the open window. "I'm glad it's only a sprain."

"I'm so sorry I lashed out at you. Please forgive me. I wish I could go back and unsay the horrible words." She put her hand on his elbow, hoping to keep him from leaving.

"There's nothing to forgive. You only said what you felt. There's no sin in being honest."

"It's not how I feel. Not anymore."

"It is, Sophie. Even if you refuse to admit it to yourself, part of you is still afraid. At first, I thought it would get better as the years passed after your father's accident. Now I know it's become a part of you."

"Kevin, no. I don't want it to be. I really don't. Can't we just say this is a spat? That I lashed out at you because I was scared for Jade, that it really has nothing to do with you or me? That it was only fear?" She choked back a sob. "I haven't been that scared since your zip-lining accident."

"I haven't broken a bone since then, Sophie." He pulled his elbow out of the window. "One day, you're going to realize that pain is a part of life. Jade had an accident. It doesn't make fun a bad thing. Fear of enjoying life will rob you of life. I'd rather live mine to the fullest than sit in a safe place, afraid, and watch it go by without me."

"There's just been too much pain. My dad, you, Logan and Caitlyn. And we didn't know how seriously Jade was injured until we saw the doctor."

"Accidents happen. You and I are responsible for teaching those two kids that they can't be afraid to live their lives just because their parents lost theirs."

"You're right. Even though I know that in my head, I still struggle with the fear."

"You need to conquer it. It's stifling to you and the kids—and me. We can't live in fear. God doesn't want us to, either."

He put the truck in gear, and she took a step back. He had every right to be upset. She couldn't force him to forgive her.

How many times had she quoted the Scripture that said God hadn't given her a spirit of fear, but of power, love and a sound mind?

She needed to change, then pray for Kevin to see it.

Chapter Twelve

Part of Kevin wanted to stay at the store until closing, but the bigger part of him wanted to see Jade. He picked up pizza on his way to the house. He didn't feel up to cooking tonight.

Jade saw him as soon as he walked through the door. "Uncle K, Carter sat on my foot and made me cry."

He shook his head. The variety of things kids could get into might never cease to amaze him. "He did?"

"It was a ac-skident." She pooched out her bottom lip. "Soapy said I had to hug him 'cause he didn't mean it. But it still hurted."

"I'm sorry. Where is he?"

"Soapy took him in the office with her."

Carter toddled out of the office. "K." He reached out his arms.

"Just a minute, little man. Let me put the pizza down." He set everything on the island and scooped the boy up with a flourish. "Have you been flying today?"

Carter giggled as Kevin flew him around the room before landing on the ottoman in front of Jade.

"I brought cheese pizza for supper. We'll eat soon."

"Yay!" Both kids clapped their hands. Relief at seeing them happy and well dispelled the gloom that had hovered over the last few hours. He'd worked, but he'd wanted to be home with them.

Sophie stuck her head out of the office. "I can help."

"I've got it. You can keep working, but it won't be long till it's ready."

He didn't know if she wanted to be around him after the day they'd had. All afternoon he'd gone over in his mind everything they'd both said. It wasn't the way he wanted them to treat one another. Jade's accident had stressed them in ways they'd never experienced. He decided to tread lightly and give her time to recover.

Parenthood took nerves of steel and strength the two of them were still developing.

"I'm between accounts anyway." She prepared the drinks while he pulled paper plates out of the pantry.

Her stiff movements let him know she wasn't okay, either. But he had news that couldn't wait until they sorted through their issues.

"Jackson called again this afternoon." He cut the kids' pizza into small bites. "Judge Carlisle had a stroke today."

"That's awful. How is he?"

Even after all the judge had done to complicate their lives, she was concerned with his well-being.

There was so much good and kind about Sophie Owens. Even on her worst days.

"They aren't sure. His wife found him at home and called an ambulance." He grabbed Carter from the sofa, where he'd climbed up to sit by Jade and put him in the high chair. "There will be more tests. Jackson said he doesn't think he'll be able to return to the bench."

"That's really sad."

Kevin watched her while he worked to get their dinner on the table. He wondered how long it would take her to realize their circumstances had just changed dramatically. A new judge meant Judge Carlisle's personal quirks were no longer a part of their decision-making process.

She handed him a can of his favorite soft drink, then carried Jade from the sofa to her stool. She sat beside Jade and propped the child's foot in her lap.

Kevin marveled at how quickly and completely Sophie had adapted to motherhood. In a matter of weeks, caring for the kids had become second nature to her.

Jade asked to say the blessing. "Lord, thank You for pink bandages, pizza and Scoopdilyicious."

"Amen." Kevin loved this little girl. He loved Carter, too. These kids had changed his world, and he wouldn't want it any other way.

Well, maybe one other way. He'd love to have Sophie's respect—and more. But she had confirmed to him today that she still didn't take him seriously. She saw him as a risk taker. He had only himself to blame for that. Years of rambunctious adventures had the entire town thinking he'd only opened his store so he could play games for the rest of his life.

If Sophie couldn't see that he'd matured after all they'd been through together, he didn't stand a chance of anyone else believing in him. Being adventurous didn't make him careless. He took risks. It was a big part of his job and life. Exercising precautions kept him safe. He hoped Sophie realized that soon.

He resigned himself to doing his best for Jade and Carter and letting the rest of it go. He couldn't control what others thought, no matter how much he longed for them to see him for who he really was.

Sophie interrupted his thoughts. "What does this mean for us? Did Jackson have any more to say about it?"

Here was her out. His next words would give Sophie all she needed to ask him to be her friend and co-parent the kids without any other relationship with him. "He said the county board of commissioners has called an emergency meeting for tomorrow. They'll name a replacement who will serve out the balance of Judge Carlisle's term. That person will take over all of his cases."

"Does that mean we have to start over?" She looked worried.

"He said one of the commissioners told him who they expect to choose, and it won't be an issue at all. It's unlikely the new judge would press for us to move beyond guardianship so quickly."

They'd managed so well with the kids—and each other—for so long. Until that kiss.

That wonderful kiss.

The kiss that had sent them into their respective corners like boxers who'd risked more than was safe and needed a break to refocus.

And then Jade got hurt.

He cleared his throat, not wanting to tell her the rest. He didn't want her to pull away from him, and she might after his next words. "He also said that no other judge would have insisted we be a couple."

Her eyes darted up to meet his and then back to her pizza. "Really?"

"Yes." Kevin lost his appetite. He picked up his plate and slid it into the trash. "I'll take care of the kids. You can go back to work. I know you missed a lot of your time this afternoon."

"Okay." Her voice was barely more than a whisper. She came around the island and threw away her plate. "I know you're still angry with me." She kept her back to the kids, he supposed in an effort to keep them from hearing her.

"Actually, I'm not angry. I was at first—not anymore." He could barely breathe with the tension between them.

"So, how do we get past this? We promised to be honest with each other. We have to fix this. I don't know what to do."

"Neither do I." He hated the helpless look in her eye, but in the same way that she was afraid of pain caused by risk, he was over opening himself up to rejection. It hurt too much.

He shrugged. "Jade will be better in a few days. I'm not sure we will."

Not knowing what else to say, he turned away from her and told the kids it was time to read a book. He wiped Carter's hands and took the tray off the high chair.

The sadness of the day broke him. Rejection was his Achilles' heel.

Until he caught a glimpse of Sophie's face when she entered the office and turned to close the door. The tears that wet her cheeks were his responsibility.

In that moment he discovered something that hurt him more than any rejection, true or perceived, he'd ever experienced. Sophie's sadness.

How had he not realized that protecting his own heart would end up hurting her? They worked together for the kids but kept pulling back from one another.

Her fear of danger and risk was so at odds with his character that he hadn't thought about how the rewards for taking a risk helped conquer his fears.

Would she be willing to take a risk on him if she saw how rewarding their lives could be if they let down their guards and became a real family?

Could she forgive him for the sadness he'd heaped on her while trying to protect himself from her rejection?

Was it too late?

The end to their temporary engagement rushed toward them in the form of a new court date.

I don't know how to make this right, Lord.

But he was going to figure it out. No matter how long it took.

The thought of the new judge and the impending possibility that Sophie might decide she didn't need to be engaged to him anymore grew larger on the horizon.

He might not have as long as it would take.

Sophie called her mother as soon as Kevin left the house that night. He'd tucked the kids in without her and texted after he left, telling her he'd locked the door and would see the kids the next morning.

"Mom." She couldn't stop the tears that filled her voice.

"What's the matter? Is Jade okay?" Her mother had embraced her role as grandparent and jumped at the first reason Sophie might call her in tears.

"She's fine." Sophie wiped away her tears with a tissue. "I didn't mean to frighten you. I need your advice."

"Tell him you love him."

"What?" Her mother had a way of cutting to the

core of a situation, but Sophie hadn't told her why she'd called.

"Tell him you love him. This is about the awkward coldness between the two of you after you took Jade to the ER. He needs to know you love him. That will get you both through whatever happened." The line was silent for a moment. "In my opinion, it's the only thing that will get you through it."

"But he's still the same. He's determined to raise the kids to be fearless. I want them to be brave, but we need to teach them caution, too."

"Sophie, I love you. You are my heart. But you're wrong. You have been since your father passed."

"Mom, you're not helping. We lost so much when we lost Dad. And Kevin is just like him."

That was the real problem. Kevin was like her father. He was brave and daring, full of life and energy. The kind of man who'd embrace life, lean into it and squeeze out every last drop of the joy it held. Every day was an adventure to him. And she'd abandoned that and let fear grip her soul.

"He is, isn't he?" Her mom chuckled softly.

"I blew it. I hurt him so badly that he'll hardly look at me, much less talk to me. I don't know that he'll ever listen to me again. It's too late. We're not young and naive like before. Now we know what life brings. The pain, the loss, the hardships. There's joy, too." She remembered Kevin's words about joy. "It's just that sometimes the joy is drowned out by the sorrow."

"Well, honey, I don't know what to tell you about falling in love and when you've missed your chance. I do know it's not about how old you are. It's about how open your heart is."

"I'm trying to open mine, but I'm afraid."

"I miss your father every day. At first it was gut wrenching. I'd hide in my room and cry my heart out. Then one day, I decided to pour my heart out to God about it. It wasn't long before I started remembering the little things he did that made me laugh. I'd see a picture or catch the scent of his cologne in the closet and I'd smile. I cherish those memories that, in the beginning, had been buried in the pain."

"Mom, I'm so sorry you had to go through that."

"I wouldn't have skipped the love to avoid the pain. Some of the best relationships, the ones where we love the deepest, are born out of pain. Like motherhood. Having you was painful, and I'd do it all over again to have you in my life—because I love you."

"Oh, Mom, I love you, too."

"I know you hate that the children lost their parents. We all do. It's tragic. But out of that pain, you became a mother. Pain is how you got your kids."

"I hadn't looked at it like that." She didn't know how she'd become so consumed with pain and grief. "I've got to let go of the pain and relish the joy."

"Tell him."

Sophie laughed. "Okay, Mom. I'll tell him. As soon as I can figure out how to get him to talk to me again. Or at least listen."

"I'll be praying for both of you."

"Thank you."

"Now go to bed. We've both got to work tomorrow."

Sophie smiled as she disconnected the call and sent up a silent prayer of thanks for her wise mother.

Help me to be like her.

* * *

The two weeks that led up to the hearing were awkward. She and Kevin had come to a truce of sorts. They worked together with the kids, even though she couldn't figure out where their relationship stood.

Every morning she prayed for the opportunity to share her heart with him like her mother had advised, and every night she went to bed wondering if she'd missed a moment to open the door of communication.

She hated the distance between them. He was close enough to touch, yet too far away to reach.

Her work schedule tightened as tax season began in earnest. Kevin's store was ramping up for the sales that preceded spring weather, causing him to put in more hours. They'd almost settled into old-married-couple mode.

She didn't know what to say to him. He laughed and joked with her and the kids, and came every morning and night as agreed. They shared meals and chores, yet neither of them talked about their future.

Good-night kisses and chats over coffee after the kids were in bed ended. She missed them. Kevin avoided any time alone with her.

Normally a very relaxed person, he now seemed as anxious as she was. Maybe they were both worried about the new judge. They'd seen enough go wrong to keep them from being overly confident.

She hoped getting beyond the stress of the legal issues would help. Maybe then he'd stop avoiding her. She prayed it wouldn't be much longer.

The new judge agreed to handle Sophie and Kevin's guardianship as scheduled. They would meet with Jackson at the courthouse. He had assured them it would all

go smoothly and wouldn't take more than a few minutes. His assurances didn't slow her constant prayers.

Kevin called early on the morning of the hearing and
apologized. He told her he couldn't come to the house to
help with the kids before court. Her mother had taken
the day off work to watch Jade and Carter for them, so
it wasn't a problem.

Or she hadn't thought it was until she heard a repeating tap echoing through the courthouse hall. She turned
and saw Kevin coming toward her on crutches.

She rushed to him. "Are you okay? What happened?
You were fine yesterday. Sit here." She pointed to a
leather bench against one wall in the wide hall.

"Relax. I'm fine." He stopped in front of the courtroom doors and leaned his weight on the crutches, keeping his left foot off the ground.

"What happened?"

"Don't worry. I'm fine."

"Were you trying out some new equipment? Did you
go back to work after you put the kids to bed last night?
Why didn't you tell me?"

"No and yes. Because I know how upset you get when
someone gets hurt."

His calm demeanor in the face of her concern didn't
surprise her. It was as if he never worried about himself. Well, she'd worry about him. For the rest of her life.

It came with the territory of admitting to herself how
much she loved him.

"How bad is it? Who took you to the ER? You did
go to the ER?"

Kevin reached out and captured her hand when it flew
back and forth close to his face as she talked. "Chad took
me to the ER. It's a sprain, only it will take a few more

days than Jade's did to heal." He looked embarrassed. "I tripped over my own feet and fell off the curb on the way to my truck last night. It was an accident, not an unnecessary risk." He released her hand and pivoted on the crutches to face the courtroom entrance.

"I'm glad you're okay." She bit her lips together to keep from saying anything else. He was safe, and she was grateful. She couldn't contain a slight chuckle at the thought of what had happened.

"Stop it." Although he didn't look at her, she could see the corner of his mouth twitch with his effort to keep from laughing with her. "And you're going to have to explain the intensity of all those rapid-fire questions to me some time in the near future."

Jackson opened the door and motioned for them.

Twenty minutes later it was done. Euphoria took over after all the weeks of worry and fear.

Kevin tapped his way out of the courtroom behind her. She stopped in the hallway with him.

"I can't catch my breath. After everything it was that easy?" She put a hand to her throat and felt the rapid beat of her pulse.

"Jackson did his homework, and the new judge isn't trying to promote a personal agenda." He leaned on the crutches again.

"They're ours. Both of them. Both of us." She pointed from herself to him and back at herself.

"Without conditions." His soberness snatched her down from her celebration.

"What are you saying?" A cavernous ache formed in her chest.

"That you were smart to say we should just be engaged. I was being my rash self when I suggested we get married on the spur of the moment like that." His even tone showed appreciation for her idea. An idea that had been motivated by her fear.

"So, you want to end the engagement?" She hadn't told him she loved him. If he ended their commitment, she could never tell him.

"I'm saying we don't have to stay engaged to keep the kids now."

"Do you think we did the right thing? Really?" Sophie wondered what gave her the idea that she and Kevin could pledge their lives to one another in the first place. Being in any relationship with him, even a temporary one, was a risk.

"Why did you do it?" His voice was serious and steady.

She shrugged one shoulder. "For the kids."

"Do you think the kids need us any less now than they did when we stood in front of Judge Carlisle and promised to make a home for them?"

"No, but is this the best way? You said we don't have to stay engaged now."

"I said we don't have to be engaged for the sake of the kids." Kevin took her hand in his callused one and drew his thumb in a pattern across her knuckles. His touch was gentle and slow. The exact opposite of everything she'd convinced herself he was.

"Sophie, I think it is the best way. I didn't just make a promise about Carter and Jade the last time we were here in court." He stilled his thumb and pressed her hand in both of his, leaning on the crutches to keep him upright. "When I told Judge Carlisle we were together, I didn't know how true it was. Even if we agreed the engagement would be temporary, in my heart I made a promise to you. A commitment to be there when you needed me. No matter what.

"After a lot of prayer the night before we first came to court, I knew I'd do whatever it took to bring the four of us together as a family. I had no idea it would mean so much more than co-parenting. It's a promise I want to keep."

In her wildest dreams, she'd never imagined their roles would shift—that she'd be the one whose mind was all over the place while Kevin kept a steady course on a path neither of them could have foreseen on the day they'd come to look after the kids so Logan and Caitlyn could go to dinner and a movie.

Kevin had faced every obstacle with strength and determination. She was the one who had fought her doubts every day. She was the one who'd struggled with her emotions.

Kevin tugged on her hand, and she went willingly into his embrace.

It was as if he knew the comforting protection she found there would settle her nerves and calm her fears.

She rested her head against his heartbeat and knew she was home.

He held her for a long moment before lifting her chin and staring deeply into her soul. "Life is worth the risk." He tucked her hair behind her ear and caressed her cheek. "Love is worth the risk, Sophie."

"Then I have something I need to tell you."

"I'm listening."

"I love you. I don't think I ever stopped loving you. The fear hid it from me, but it was there, buried in my heart, waiting for you to find it."

"I love you, Sophie Owens. Will you stay engaged to

me? For real? Like the kind of engaged where we actually get married?"

She wrapped her arms around him, and the crutches crashed to the floor with a thunderous echo. "If you promise it won't be a long engagement. I don't care for long engagements."

Kevin's kiss held a promise that all they'd come through together had indeed made them a family.

Epilogue

Kevin waited in the front of the courtroom for Sophie. He held Carter in his arms. The tiny suit he wore matched Kevin's. The doors opened, and Jade walked in wearing a pink dress that was everything a princess could desire. A tiny tiara was nestled in her golden curls. She carried a basket with Rosie and Sissy tucked among flowers. Jade strewed the petals onto the wooden floor as she made her way to the front of the room.

Sophie followed her with one hand linked through her mother's arm.

She was a vision of loveliness. The white lace dress with pearls showed her beauty to perfection. Her dark hair was twisted up in soft, intricate waves. Her tiara matched Jade's.

With special permission from the new judge, Pastor Gillis began the ceremony, and Diane settled with the children on the front row of the courtroom.

Kevin heard every word spoken and responded when asked, but his entire being was consumed by the woman at his side. They exchanged vows and rings.

"You may kiss the bride."

"I love you, Sophie Lane." He caught Jade's attention. "Are you watching, Jade?"

"Kiss her, Uncle K." Jade threw the rest of her flowers into the air around them.

Laughter filled the court as he lowered his face to Sophie's. He kissed her sweet smile with a heart full of love. The kiss she returned echoed his joy. Nothing he'd ever done thrilled him more than being in this moment.

As soon as the wedding ceremony ended, the judge invited the children to join Kevin and Sophie at the table in the front of the courtroom. They signed the papers Jackson had prepared to finalize the adoption and their new names.

Judge Stewart added her seal and signature to the papers. She smiled at Jade and Carter.

"I'm so glad I got to meet you, Jade Elise West Lane and Carter Logan West Lane. Did you know that this paper I signed means these are your new parents?"

Jade shook her head. "They're not new. Mommy and Daddy got them for us."

"I see." The judge looked just as impressed with Jade as Kevin was. "Can you tell me something then? Since they gave you new names, what are you going to call them?"

"Mommy and Daddy. 'Cause that's their job. Mommy and Daddy gave us to them so they can take care of us."

"I think that's wonderful." Judge Stewart smiled and waved goodbye to the kids.

Sophie tugged on Kevin's hand. "I think the judge needs her courtroom back." She pointed as Judge Stewart walked around the end of the bench.

He was a married man with two children, and he couldn't be happier. Or more scared. This new life chal-

lenged him in ways he hadn't foreseen. And he'd face it
with the faith he'd relied on to get him to this day.

Kevin herded his new family to the SUV and drove
them to the church for their wedding reception.

In the fellowship hall, their friends clapped and
cheered when Pastor Gillis introduced them.

An hour later, exhausted and happier than he'd ever
been, Kevin sat at the head table with Sophie. The kids
played with their classmates under the watchful eye of
their new grandmother.

"I want to show you something." He leaned in close
with an arm around the back of her chair and took her
left hand in his. "You already know I asked your dad
for your hand, and he said yes, but made me promise to
wait until after you graduated."

Sophie nodded. "Mom told me when we got engaged."

Their lives had changed so much since that day. All
for the better.

"I didn't just buy the engagement ring. I also bought
the wedding band and had it engraved. I wanted you to
see the message inside today, on the day we start our
life together."

She slipped the ring from her finger and read it aloud.
"'My favorite adventure.'" Tears filled her eyes.

He'd meant every word all those years ago, but the
sentiment was richer and sweeter now. Life had taught
him Sophie's true value.

"I want you to know that you've always been the one
I'd risk anything and everything for."

She cupped his cheeks and kissed his lips. "I love you,
Kevin." She dabbed at her eyes with a tissue. "I have a
secret about your ring, too."

He took it off without waiting for her to tell the story. *Love is Worth the Risk*. It was his turn to kiss her.

"That was my father's ring. I've worn it on a chain since he passed. Mom wanted me to have it to remember him by. It symbolized his commitment to making a family with her. I chose to give it to you in honor of that sentiment. I'm committed to you, and to our family."

Her eyes glistened with unshed tears. "To know that my father approved of you as my husband is something I'll always treasure. It wouldn't have happened if you hadn't taken that risk when we were so young."

"You've taken the biggest leap of all. You married me." He caressed her cheek and sent a silent prayer of thanks to God that this amazing woman was his wife.

Diane brought Carter over and passed him to Sophie. "I'll be over at the cake table if you need me."

Jade ran up and jumped into Kevin's lap. She wrapped her arms around his neck. "Are you gonna stay at our house now?"

He straightened her tiara, loving how she was enjoying the day as much as he and Sophie were. "I am."

Sophie laced her fingers with his and drew the kids into a circle with them. "We're a family. Family stays together."

Carter clapped his hands. "Dada. Home."

Jade's brow wrinkled. "You're the daddy now, but you still gots to be the cooker."

Sophie dissolved into giggles. "Jade, do you think Daddy could teach me to cook, too?"

Jade tapped her chin with one finger and thought about it. "No, 'cause you're not a good cooker." She reached up to kiss Sophie's cheek. "But it's okay. You're a princess like me."

"She sure is." Kevin looked into Sophie's loving eyes and saw the bravest woman he'd ever know.

* * * * *

If you enjoyed this book, pick up these other sweet romances from Love Inspired.

The Baby Next Door
by Vannetta Chapman

The Amish Teacher's Wish
by Tracey J. Lyons

Rebuilding Her Life
by Ruth Logan Herne

A True Cowboy
by Danica Favorite

Her Secret Hope
by Lorraine Beatty

Find more great reads at www.LoveInspired.com

Dear Reader,

Sometimes the challenges of life come out of nowhere and turn our world upside down. Kevin and Sophie lost their dearest friends, and both of them gave up their way of life to care for Jade and Carter.

Death is hard, and the people left behind must deal with the changes loss brings.

But sometimes the hardest challenges we face come from within. Confronting our fears, opening up our wounded hearts, learning to trust God and even—on occasion—recommitting to trusting people who've betrayed us in the past. These can be the things that make or break us.

Kevin and Sophie conquered all of their challenges to build a better life for themselves. A life they'd given up on.

I pray you're willing to open your heart to whatever God sends your way. Whether it's a dream you've long ago given up on or a new dream you could never have imagined.

Life with Christ is an adventure. Enjoy the journey.

I'd love to hear from you. Connect with me at www. angelmoorebooks.com, where you'll find links to all my books, the latest news and my social media. You can also sign up for my newsletter on the home page.

God bless you.
Angel Moore

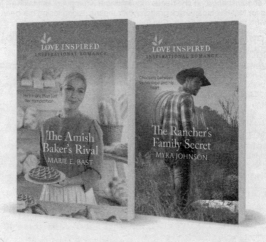

Get 4 FREE REWARDS!

We'll send you 2 FREE Books plus 2 FREE Mystery Gifts.

Love Inspired books feature uplifting stories where faith helps guide you through life's challenges and discover the promise of a new beginning.

FREE Value Over $20